BANSHEES, BOOMBOXES, AND BONES

BEWITCHER'S BEACH PARANORMAL COZY MYSTERIES
MYSTERIES
BOOK 4

EMILY FLUKE

ALSO BY EMILY FLUKE

Be sure to snag the prequels to both the Mari Fable Mysteries, and the Bewitcher's Beach Paranormal Cozy Mysteries FREE from my newsletter: The Glass Coffin and Be Careful What You Witch For.

https://landing.mailerlite.com/webforms/landing/y4h6c8

To Colin, for always showing up for me.

CAST OF CHARACTERS

Noema Wolf (temporary last name) Once werewolves are turned, they have no memory of their previous lives.

As a werewolf who can smell emotions and a lover of mystery movies, Noema finds herself sniffing out suspects whenever a troublesome visitor upsets her cozy, seaside town. But another case is not what this single mother of four, manager of Mockbuster Video Rental, and playwright needs thrown into her busy schedule.

Halen, Dio, Jovi, and Stevie Wolf:

These four mischievous 'pups' each help their mom solve mysteries or run the video rental shop in their own unique ways. As born werewolves, they don't experience memory loss —but as eight-year-olds, they suffer selective hearing when it comes to following the rules.

Sheriff Sett Lawrence:

This overprotective gargoyle takes life too seriously. His six-foot, six-inch stony body with muscular wings and horns does nothing to match his introverted, patient, and studious personality. But it certainly frightens visitors.

Crow:

A mysterious man with a handsome smirk. Crow took advantage of the low housing market in Bewitcher's Beach after a newcomer was recently murdered. This "tall dark" has plenty of secrets but isn't afraid to tease, flirt, and joke in the face of danger. And as hidden as he may seem—as the new owner of Roller Shakes—Crow socializes with the whole town on a regular basis.

Hattie Sharpe:

This harsh, flapper-girl starlet became a ghost in the height of the Roaring Twenties when her bold attitude landed her the target of a deadly Hollywood stunt. Now, she directs Everland Theater's plays and tells it like it is, no matter how many enemies it creates.

Senna James:

A senior student at Shadowvale University and one of Noema's friends. Senna is as skilled at being a witch as she is fashionable.

Madam Rowena:

The chief academic officer at Shadowvale, Madam Rowena, is both harsh and brilliant. She may be a little harsh and a lot strict, but at least she gets the respects she believes she deserves.

Carissa Harbour (Coach):

Lovingly called 'Coach' by everyone at the university, she is one of the most powerful witches to have existed in modern history. Coach is both the dean of Shadowvale, and she's dead. How can she run a school from the afterlife? She's also a ghost who haunts the campus.

CHAPTER 1
READ THE ROOM

NORTHERN CALIFORNIA, WINTER 1998

SMELLING people's emotions came with a hefty dose of drama and the constant temptation to diagnose the source of every smell. Like did all four of my children stink of rotten fish because they rolled around on the beach while in their wolf forms? Or were they all in on a collective lie that sparked the stench of guilt? I narrowed my eyes at the row of eight-year-olds, who each swore they didn't roll in the sand. The trail of wet footprints and specks of sand sprinkled across the shop's gray carpet said otherwise.

I frowned and folded my arms. "What did I say?"

My daughter's wolf ears flicked back. Each child resembled me, with a piece of their werewolf self lingering while in human form. But because of her ears, Stevie mirrored me the most. She raised her hand as if this was a classroom and not the video rental shop she was growing up in. She cleared her throat, ready to present an argument. "You said not to get dirty before the long drive."

"That's right—"

Stevie's wolf ears perked up and she poked a finger into the air, speaking over me. "But we didn't play in the dirt. So when

Dio said we all had to cross our fingers behind our backs to make the lie not a lie, I said no way. Because we don't need to lie since we didn't break the rule. Sand isn't dirt." She shrugged and pursed her lips in a cheeky grin.

Raucous laughter echoed from behind me. I shot a murderous look over my shoulder at both my ghost best friend and the guy I was pseudo-dating. My narrowed eyes did nothing to faze their amusement. Hattie's form flickered as she glanced at Crow and stifled another round of giggles. The 1920s flapper girl-turned-ghost looked like the perfect complement to the tall, dark, and rakish reaper who stood beside her at the end of the aisle of horror videos.

"What?" Hattie mimicked Stevie's shrug. "She's got you there."

Crow's perpetually disheveled hair fell into his face as he leaned closer to Hattie. He cracked a sideways grin, keeping his eyes on me as he spoke. "Noema's bark is worse than her bite, right? I'm pretty sure she's going to bite my head off since she can't get to you."

I pointed two fingers at my eyes and then back at the two troublemakers as if to say "I'm watching you." Though I wasn't actually mad at anyone. The mixed smell of key lime pie and ammonia came from hope and nerves swirling in my gut. Today, I might finally get answers.

Hattie waved a wispy, transparent hand. The movement had her fringe dress glittering. "Please keep the biting talk to the bedroom."

"Hattie!" I said through my teeth. "Can you not?" I discreetly shifted my wide eyes back and forth. From her, to the row of kids who caught every word of her joke, and then back to her. Thankfully, they weren't privy to the suggestiveness behind it, and anyway, there was absolutely none of that going on. Crow and I were as casual as a Friday dress code. We'd kissed all of one time before he decided to take on new responsibilities as a reaper of the dead. Since traveling was in his near future and I was happy in our small seaside town, we'd decided not to label whatever this spark was between us. At least, not until we could figure out the logistics of dating long distance for weeks at a time.

"So we're not in trouble, right?" Stevie asked. She tapped her wrist where a broken *101 Dalmatians* watch clung to her arm. "Because I still have to pack my snack bag for the field trip and I don't have time for a timeout."

I palmed my face and sighed. In exactly one hour, we had to meet up with the other parents and chaperones at Bewitcher's Beach Elementary for a field trip to Shadowvale University, a magical college that was both as famous as it was mysterious. The faculty preferred to keep it that way since witches, werewolves, ghosts, and reapers still freaked some people out. Even though they had known about us for several decades, and most of us didn't exactly *hide* anymore. Some of the biggest scaredy cats became hunters, deeming themselves vigilantes against magic-wielding or supernatural people like us. Of course, hunting and killing anyone was illegal. We'd fully assimilated into society over the past thirty years, but it didn't mean everyone accepted us.

I waved the kids toward the staircase at the back of the shop that led to our loft above. "Just go pack your snacks."

Eight thundering feet pounded up the steps as they pushed and shoved to be the first one home. They argued over who'd get the last pack of Dunkaroos. I ignored the bickering and shuffled around the front desk to stare at a squat computer that doubled as the shop's register. I hit the power button and waited for the screen to warm up before plopping onto the stool. Leaning forward, I folded my arms on the desk and made eye contact with Hattie, who was quietly scolding Crow.

"Don't talk about what you don't understand," she said.

Crow shoved his hands into the pockets of his black jeans. "I'm just saying, it doesn't make sense that a ghost could get carsick. Your stomach is literally always empty."

"I'm sick every time I get a load of that hogwash you drown yourself in. Does *that* make enough sense for you?"

"That's just my natural musk."

Hattie threw her head back and laughed. "Right. Because you naturally smell like you took a bath in a pool of Calvin Klein Eternity."

He gave her a deadpan stare, but his crooked mouth betrayed his faux anger. They bickered like they were the ones dating. The scent of my confusion swirled around me with the unsettling smell of pineapple pizza. For a moment, I swore I saw a literal spark ignite between my best friend and...man... friend, but it was just Hattie's golden dress catching the glint of the overhead lights with every ripple of movement.

I blinked and gave my wolf ears a little shake. "So are we carpooling?" Crow and Hattie both snapped their attention to me and nodded. Relief flooded me. Now I had an excuse not to ride the bus with the kids.

I didn't want to sit stifled by two dozen elementary school kids' emotions for the three hour drive to Shadowvale. Hattie planned to visit a friend at the university, and Crow had tossed around the idea of riding with us since it was halfway to his next destination as a reaper. He was supposed to check in with another reaper and decide on territorial lines for their duties. Whenever someone passed away within their respective borders, it became their responsibility to guide that person's spirit to the afterlife. "Okay, I'm leaving to drop the kids off at school so they can ride the bus with their friends. Then I'll swing back by the shop to grab you guys."

When the computer screen finally came to life, I signed

into the register so that Hattie's daughter could run the rental shop while I was gone.

"We'll go to the dropoff with you," Hattie said. "I'm taking any chance I get to haunt you about that screenplay." Her pointed look sent nerves rippling through me. Long ago, I'd made a promise to write a screenplay worthy of the big screen. We only had three months and four days until remodeling began. Our small town stage was about to transform into a big screen, and I'd sworn to Hattie that I'd complete my screenplay before them. That way I could pitch it to the agents she'd invite to the grand opening. At the very least, I owed her a promise kept after she'd gone through the trouble to contact her friends in Hollywood for me.

Crow nodded along, but a flush of regret wafted from him, pulling me from my thoughts. The smell of toast left to cook too long burned in the air and temporarily washed out the scent of his cologne.

I tilted my head, eyeing him. "Are you sure you're okay with this?"

He scrubbed the back of his neck. "I'm just not great around kids. The snotty noses, you know. I always think they're going to get me sick."

I couldn't blame the guy. After seeing death on the regular, it made sense he feared even a little mucus. Kids had a way of coughing directly into your soul.

"It's why I haven't decided if I want to stop in for the Shadowvale tour."

I stood and skirted around the desk. Giving Crow's hand a squeeze, I said, "You guys can stay in the car at the elementary school. But I hope you come on the Shadowvale tour with us."

"And I wish you could come on this trip with me," he said, dark eyes nearly swallowing me whole. He returned the hand squeeze and then released me, reaching up to push a curl from my face. Our eyes locked in a moment of wishful thinking. Him wanting me to come with him. Me wishing he'd stay living here. Despite Hattie's proximity, he leaned in, and my heart skipped at the possibility of an unexpected kiss.

The bell above the shop's door chimed, and I dropped my hold on Crow and stepped back. A gargoyle clad in a navy police officer uniform ducked through the door. Sett usually stopped by to grab a pack of orange-flavored Creme Savers, or just to say hi, but today, the crease between his brow sent my heart skittering. I thought I'd gotten used to his serious outlook on life. Sett deemed himself protector of all, and his letter-of-the-law attitude was often mistaken for grumpiness.

His slate eyes passed over Crow and Hattie and landed on me. Sett marched across the shop toward me and, stepping close, gently cupped my upper arm. "Noema, I have some news." I rarely caught the scent of Sett's emotions buried beneath his thick, stony skin, but I didn't need to now. Sett wore his worry in the hard line of his mouth.

My heart sank and I folded my wolf ears back, pressing them against my thick curls. Together, we'd solved more than one murder in the last three months. The thought of more bad news sickened me. "What happened?"

He glanced at Crow and Hattie and then cleared his throat. "*The Book of Prophecies* is gone."

Every muscle in my body went rigid. I didn't move, didn't blink. After an indeterminate passage of thick silence, I forced a laugh and raked my fingers through my hair. They caught on my curls until I tugged my hand out. "For a second I thought you said *The Book of Prophecies* was missing." A strange laugh tumbled out of me again as I looked at Crow and Hattie.

Their eyes were wide, and Hattie shook her head. "Oh, Doll. I know those wolf ears don't need their hearing checked. You're in denial."

Sett closed his eyes for a moment. He gave my arm a little squeeze and then offered a grim smile that didn't look right on his cold, pensive face. "Your friend, Senna, called me and asked me to break the news to you before you came to Shadowvale. It happened a few days ago, but she wanted me to wait until the last minute to tell you in case they located it. She knew it'd break your heart."

"That's not possible," I said. "The witches guard that grimoire better than gold. It's literally one of the most important documents in the history of magic."

And I'd found it. After the book had been lost for decades, I'd found it. Right here in town, I'd sniffed out the grimoire buried in a hidden compartment at Bewitcher's Beach Public Library. Since then, whenever I came in contact with the old book, a rush of peculiar smells sent me into a haze of forgotten memories. Forgotten because, as a turned werewolf, I couldn't remember my life before fangs and fur. No turned werewolf could, but most didn't lose their families and identities in the process. When I became a wolf at sixteen, I lost everything— until I found *The Book of Prophecies*.

Absent-mindedly, I yanked at the stretched-out collar of my hoodie and traced the little mark that looked like a tattoo of wings on my skin. It appeared only a couple of months ago. The mark proved I was part of a prophecy written in the grimoire. A prophecy that I hoped would lead me to the family and identity I ached to know. But I didn't understand the strange poetic words of witches from long ago, so I needed Shadowvale's help to interpret it. We all needed Shadowvale's help after a spell protecting Bewitcher's Beach was mysteriously stripped away and crime rates rose all over town.

When the witches procured *The Book of Prophecies*, they promised to study it, working to recreate a protection spell that once shielded our town from harm. The magic quite literally stopped attackers in their tracks, which had created a safe haven for all supernatural people. I was desperate to get there and ask what they'd learned from the worn pages full of magic and prophetic text. But as desperate as I'd felt, I tempered my impatience because the witches had their work cut out for them and I was instructed by the chief academic officer of Shadowvale to give them space. So I'd waited until my children were invited there on a field trip. It caused a great deal of stress, all that waiting, but I'd done it both as a test of my patience and to let the witches work their magic without my nose in the way.

I swallowed and faked a smile. "It doesn't matter. This is fine. Everything is fine. I found it once before. No big deal."

Sett searched my face, not letting go of my arm. "Noema, the good news is that they took a lot of notes before the grimoire went missing, and they've already reported a possible theft so their police department is involved."

"Perfect. That's great."

By the look on his face, he knew it wasn't perfect, or great. Sett knew me better than that, and he said as much. "I know notes won't help you jog your memory the way the original book did. But maybe it'll be enough until the detective tracks it down. I just worry you'll be stressed about it until then."

Crow stepped up beside me, his shoulder bumping mine and knocking Sett's hand off of me. "I've got it from here, Officer," Crow said, addressing him formally as if he didn't know Sett. "I'll worry about Noema for you." I slid my gaze to him, catching a smoky scent mixed with body odor—irritation and jealousy. "I'm going with her to Shadowvale."

My pulse skipped, and when he glanced at me, I gave him a small smile. His news melted a bit of the tension in my muscles, and my cheeks heated with delight that we'd get more time together before he left.

Despite Crow now standing inside Sett's personal space,

the three of us crowded together, Sett didn't step back. He lifted his other arm, the one Crow didn't bump into, and gave my bicep another quick squeeze. "Don't do anything crazy; the cops there don't know you like I do. Let the detective do his job and don't get involved."

"We won't be in your jurisdiction, Officer, so I don't see how you need to worry about it," Crow said. This strange little tiff was getting to be about as annoying as when my kids squabbled. Yes, I'd almost dated Sett. Yes, I was semi-dating Crow now. And yes, I was friends with both of them. They needed to get the heck over it and act like grown men.

Sett frowned. "I'm not just Noema's sheriff, I'm her friend. And as a friend, I worry—"

I threw my hands up, effectively pushing them both away. "How about nobody worries? I sniffed out the grimoire once before and I'll do it again. Capiche?"

Nobody dared say anything. The growl in my voice must have gotten my point across. Maybe I *would* bite. I had a three hour car ride and a full day of chaperoning thirty 8-year-olds ahead of me, and I hadn't even had my morning Diet Pepsi yet.

I marched to the stairs, yelled for the kids, and shooed everyone out of the shop within a matter of minutes. I refused to waste another second. Not while *The Book of Prophecies* was missing.

CHAPTER 2
GHOSTLY ALUMNI

APPROXIMATELY TWO HUNDRED MINUTES LATER, I hopped out of our old Astro van, landing on the gravel drive outside Shadowvale University. I tilted my head back and soaked in an array of smells.

The decay of fallen leaves buried in perpetual dampness.

The acidic warmth of a cappuccino.

And the bite of...was that tequila? This was a college campus, and though I'd never attended university, I'd seen enough movies to suspect these were the scents of parties and hangover coffees. Shadowvale's gothic architecture didn't look anything like the brick colleges I'd seen on TV where young adults played catch on the lawn or gossiped in cliques. I scanned the campus for Senna, my friend who'd visited Bewitcher's Beach only two months back. I spotted two young warlocks tossing a fabric bag into the air. When I didn't see a beautiful young witch among them, I turned my attention to the Main Hall.

Shadowvale's main building was a cross between the pictures I'd seen of the University of Notre Dame and the Canterbury Cathedral. Towering, intimidating, and gloomy, but glorious enough that I couldn't look away. I didn't even want to blink. Statues of gargoyles flanked the columns at the front entrance, and nearly a hundred narrow stained-glass windows lined the first floor. A massive sign stood to the right of the base of the steps. Etched in stone, it read "Shadowvale University Main Hall." To the left, three identical buildings formed a hook shape at one end of the courtyard, and closer to the Main Hall stood a library that matched the Victorian gothic.

I took another long sniff, hoping to catch a hint of the grimoire like the day I found it at the Bewitcher's Beach library. *The Book of Prophecies* smelled of sugar and spice and everything I'd sacrificed since becoming a werewolf—the home and family I imagined in my daydreams. Though I couldn't remember if turning into a werewolf was my choice or not, considering I didn't even remember turning.

I scraped my memory for the grimoire's unique scent. The cinnamon sweetness of holidays and fragrant rose perfume. The slightest whiff of sweetness left my mouth watering and heart throbbing for the sight and comfort of the familiar grimoire. I may have imagined the saccharine scent buried beneath all the other smells, or it could have come from syrupy coffee creamers. I didn't have long enough to discern the scent before Bewitcher's Beach elementary school's bus rolled up and puffed diesel fuel into the air.

I deflated along with the hissing sound of the bus's brakes. Once the kids loaded back into the bus at the end of the day, then I'd speak with the chief academic officer at Shadowvale. Madam Rowena was the witch who procured *The Book of Prophecies* when it left Bewitcher's Beach. She oversaw the study of the grimoire while the school's dean had the final say. She'd know the details about how and when it went missing.

Kids piled out of the bus, stumbling over one another to

race around the gravel or gape at the gargoyle statues that looked twice as large and thrice as frightening as a real gargoyle. A sudden sharp odor assaulted my nose. I nearly gagged at the burn of ammonia—the smell of fear. I'd come in contact with it around murders and suspects before, so my pulse skittered and my ears folded back.

Crow came up behind me with his nose pinched. Even Hattie waved her wispy hand in front of her face.

"Do you guys smell that too?" I asked. They nodded, frowns twisting their faces in disgust while I sank with relief. This wasn't ammonia from fear. It was...I sniffed again. Pee. Yep. Somebody definitely peed their pants on the road trip.

Crow snaked his hand around my waist where it quickly dipped to my hip. My heart danced from his touch—until he opened his mouth. "I think I'm going to duck out early."

I shot him a look, my brows furrowed. Maybe my bottom lip stuck out a little too. "Already?"

He took my hand in his and brought it to his mouth. The brush of his lips over my knuckles raised my hopes until he quickly dashed them again with an apologetic look. "The regional reaper said he'd come pick me up whenever I needed. I want to stay with you, but this many kids is..." His gaze flickered over the gaggle of children shouting, making fart noises, and laughing. Someone was crying. The dark and broody reaper was entirely out of his element.

"Okay." It was all I said as we directed the students inside to use the restrooms.

Crow trudged along behind, hands in his pockets while Hattie vanished to find Jane, a ghost who haunted the school.

The floor in the Main Hall was coated with dark marble that caught the light of fairy-curated chandeliers. It brightened the university's old gothic look. Like a school of fish, we moved in sync, ducking to the left to a short hallway marked with a restroom sign. I waited outside the restroom with the few children who claimed they didn't need a toilet. A vampire boy, a human girl, and my werewolf daughter Stevie marveled at portraits of witches, warlocks, and humans who taught at Shadowvale.

The painted teacher glared down her nose at them as if scolding the boy for putting his finger on the frame. The eyes in the portrait shifted back and forth and then landed directly on the vampire.

They all squealed and ran for the opposite wall, pressing their little bodies against the windows. Once again, the pungent odor of ammonia filled my nose.

I knelt in front of them, quieting their screams. "It's just a ghost playing tricks on you." I nodded toward the portrait, which was now just a flat painting. The culprit drifted down the hall, off to haunt something else. Thankfully, the kids had plenty of ghost friends and knew they were no scarier than anyone else. But I'd read about Shadowvale's history, and some of the ghosts that haunted it had died on campus. The dean herself was a ghost called Coach whose death was shrouded in mystery. So I couldn't blame the kids for being a little spooked about deaths that happened right on the very ground where we stood.

I pointed at Stevie and her friend. "You both obviously need to use the toilet."

Stevie's eyes bugged, round and shimmering with wonder as they trailed to the haunting woman in the walls. "How did you know?"

"About the ghost?" I followed her line of sight and cocked my head. "Because this is Shadowvale! It's infamous for the alumni that haunt it. Even when students graduate, they come back because they loved it so much. That's part of why we're here today, to learn how to truly appreciate education."

Stevie shook her head, folding her wolf ears back. She was my mirror, while her three brothers carried their werewolf forms either in their feet or their voice. "No, I mean how did you know I need to pee?"

I rolled my eyes and pointed to her dancing feet and crossed legs. "Because of that."

The kids scurried to the bathroom, and I was left alone in the long hall until someone came up behind me, brushing against the back of my elbow.

"Listen," Crow said. His dark eyes sagged. "I'm going to head out. This is interesting, but I think I'll come back for a tour without the elementary school."

"Right." I nodded. *But you can't stay here for me?*

He must have sensed my disappointment because he stepped closer and planted a kiss on my forehead. "I know you'll sniff out that grimoire. You're capable of anything."

The truth in his voice matched the smell of lavender in his emotions. He believed in me. It was one of the things I liked most about Crow. Despite my tendency to find myself in a bit of trouble, he trusted I was capable and clever enough that he never truly worried about me. Not the way Sett did with his overbearing protectiveness. I stood a little taller. "Thanks. I think I may have caught a whiff of it. Or something sweet like it, at least."

He crooked a half-smile and leaned so close his breath brushed my ear. "I'll miss you."

My heart sank thinking of all the time he'd be gone traveling, learning about his expanded region and meeting with the other reapers. He was still so young in his Calling as a guide of spirits. He needed this mentorship and experience. Still, I hated that he wouldn't be in Bewitcher's Beach when we returned. Especially if I didn't find *The Book of Prophecies*. I'd want his shoulder to cry on. "Goodbye, Crow," I finally said.

He glanced side-to-side, likely checking if any little eyes were on us. In one quick movement, he pressed his lips to mine, stole my breath, and stepped back. Just like that, he was walking away and pushing through the double doors that led outside, where the other reapers would pick him up and take him away. He'd be gone for months. I swallowed, pressing gently to my lips to linger in the memory of his kiss before dropping him from my mind and focusing on the children.

After everyone emerged from the restrooms, the tour guide gathered us in the center of the Main Hall, where we were surrounded by a long, curving hallway. The hallway branched into smaller sections but completed a full and perfect circle. The woman introduced herself as a jack-of-all-trades witch, which made her the ideal registrations director. Based on the slight shimmer of scales beneath her skin and the hint of crimson in her eyes, she was also a half-dragon. The burgundy Shadowvale sweater she wore over a lacy black dress complemented her red irises.

She tossed her hair over her shoulder and led us from the lobby and back into the curved hall. Silver sprinkled through her long gray waves, and the hem of her dress dragged over the carpet like a bride's train.

"I hate to bear bad news, but we are not viewing the library today after an important grimoire went missing. In fact, a little birdy told me that your class is from the very same town where *The Book of Prophecies* was found. As you may already know, the protection spell was stolen or lost from it, but we hope to recover it. Someday we'll use the grimoire's minor shielding spells to recreate the protection."

If we found it... I opened my mouth to dig for details but thought better of it. The field trip tour wasn't the time for me to get answers. This was for the kids.

Stevie's hand shot into the air. She waved vigorously,

jumping up and down as she walked. Pigtails bounced like tiny bird wings, and I couldn't help but think Stevie looked like the finches she claimed to communicate with back home. After approximately ten seconds, she gave up waiting and shouted out. "My mom smelled the book!" The witch peaked her thin blonde brows but before she could respond, Stevie pointed at me and kept going. "Right here. That's my mom. She found it at our library. She smells everything. Sometimes things that aren't even there."

And now I sound insane. I forced an even smile to temper the twitch in my cheek.

The witch's expression confirmed what I thought. She squinted at me and seemed to be biting back a smile. "Thank you for sharing. We'll leave sharing time for the end of the tour. You're missing all kinds of interesting experiences. Look here." She waved a manicured hand at an Impressionist-inspired piece of artwork.

Swirls of ruby and lemon yellow depicted a swath of flowers blooming from a cauldron with a shield on it. Beside it sat a glass bottle full of orange liquid where a bee perched on the rim. Wind seemed to gently bend the flowers' stems.

"These paintings are timeless examples of spells that witches and warlocks here at Shadowvale have created. Seniors are required to create and complete a unique spell in order to graduate. Many of our spells are designed to help others, much like the now famous protection spell from *The Book of Prophecies*. Here, a witch from the late eighteen hundreds fashioned a tonic that was intended to relieve the pain of childbirth. She used petals from wildflowers, the intention of a honeybee, and words spoken by Norse shieldmaidens during battle. Jane's project was successful, and she graduated top of her class."

Jane? I had to ask Hattie to introduce me to her later. If it was the same Jane, I definitely wanted to meet her and thank her. It was possible I took that very same tonic during labor. My late husband and I had chosen a witch doula because we hoped the magic would spare me from the pain of delivering quadruplets.

The tour guide explained a dozen famous spells that had gone forth to make life better for every person. Preservation magic to keep food edible during droughts. Sun enchantments used to enhance electrical heaters for long winters. Even melodic charms designed to ease insomnia. I couldn't wait to ask Senna what kind of spell she was creating.

Kids became restless with the lengthy descriptions, so the witch skipped the last few paintings and led us to the exit.

"What's that room?" I asked as we passed. No placard identified the room like the other doors along the maze of hallways.

"That's Coach's office," she said as we stepped out into the scattered sunshine. "The dean of Shadowvale. She prefers to be called Coach rather than her official title, which is Dean Harbour." I glanced back as we shuffled away from the building, but the hall had already shifted. Like a Rubik's cube, it seemed to rotate downward, folding in on itself. In a blink, a new area replaced it. The front hall again. "And that movement you see is our maze magic installed decades ago to protect supernatural people from those of us who deigned to hunt us."

The children gasped and whispered, a nervous energy sweeping over them. Most of this supernatural crew was young, too young to know much about hunters, since we supernaturals had mostly assimilated into mainstream society.

She continued. "It can sense malcontent in newcomers and shift the hallways to guide them back to the entrance over and over until they give up and leave. Unfortunately, it is not foolproof. It works a bit like computer software with the need for occasional troubleshooting."

Did this tour guide forget these were third through fifth

graders? They'd immediately lost interest when she went into too much detail. Though the "shooting" line lifted a few heads as they misunderstood her meaning.

If only Shadowvale had the protection spell that once guarded Bewitcher's Beach. That was foolproof. As far as anyone knew, it never once glitched. This maze magic was impressive too, but nothing like the spells in *The Book of Prophecies*.

I sniffed deeply, hoping to catch the book's scent, but the only sweet smell drifted from where the guide pointed at a cafeteria. "We'll end our tour with a meal before you all take the long drive back home. For now, let me show you the gardens."

We exited out the back of the Main Hall and stepped into an eternal autumn. Life-size statues were scattered through a garden full of trees with orange and brown leaves. Each statue depicted an animal. Little engraved plaques sat in front of the statues, and a small fountain of water surrounded each one.

Rabbits and foxes and reindeer and—oh hey, a wolf! I smiled and walked up to the glistening stone.

The tour guide presented the wolf. "This is the mother of Madam Rowena's familiar. Myst was a fiercely loyal familiar to the wizard who bonded her, and now her pup, Mysty, is a full-grown and powerful familiar who has bonded with Madam Rowena. I hope your school has taught you about familiars, but we'll cover the basics."

The crowd of fuzzy heads leaned in like a wave, rapt with attention about the animals they might someday bond. "Familiars are animals with magic, passed down through their lineage like witches and warlocks in our ancestry. A familiar shares their magic with the person they trust the most—the witch or warlock they bond with. The witch can then siphon the familiar's magic to boost her own. Now this is what you might find most exciting. Unlike witch magic, anyone can enjoy the bene-fits of a familiar's magic if they were to bond with the familiar. The likelihood of that, however, is very very slim. Familiars choose, well, familiar people. People with magic of their own so the power can be shared both ways."

A shapeshifter boy's hand shot into the air. Something sticky shined on his fingertips, like melted peppermints. "I have a pet hamster. Can I use his power?"

A group of little girls stifled giggles. Even the tour guide had to suppress a smirk before she answered. "Pets, even highly intelligent ones, are not the same as familiars." I thought of our pet mouse, Squeaks, who seemed to understand me almost as well as another person. He communicated with chirps and even helped me break into a filing closet at the police station. But he wasn't magical, just intelligent. I missed his furry little face but had no doubt he was enjoying the company of Hattie's daughter. "Later, we'll go see where the familiars are housed. They have their own cozy dormitory, and you'll get to meet our expert on magical animals. You can ask the professor more questions about familiars then."

We moved on to swerve through a dozen more familiar statues and then out to the edge of the campus. I sucked in a breath. The air smelled of redwood trees and the dewy decom-position of damp leaves. Clouds coated the sky, only allowing the sun to cast yolky orange rays through occasional breaks. A chilly draft swirled through the outer edge of the campus as we trailed along the forest that surrounded the university. Massive redwood trees cast long shadows over most of the campus. The forest went on for as far as we could see.

A hint of sweetness mingled with the scent of redwoods. I sniffed again, pausing as the rest of the touring crew meandered on. Staring into the shrouded woods, I froze, my only move-ment the expansion of my lungs.

Was that the smell of the grimoire? Cinnamon sugar left my mouth watering. Notes of flowers carried in the breeze. My pulse skittered. I inhaled another gulp and burst into a cough at the unexpected odor of decay. Gross. Must have been from the magic that kept Shadowvale in an endless state of autumn, nature's death.

Except the forest wasn't part of the campus.

I shook my head. The smell was gone and so were the rest of the field trip participants. I hurried ahead with a glance back at the shadows hovering over the edge of the redwoods.

Later, I'd come back here and try to catch that scent again.

CHAPTER 3
CLAWS FOR CONCERN

I TRIED to listen to the tour guide, but I couldn't focus. Whoever thought up the word "patience" needed a bite in the arm. I wanted nothing more than to run back to the forest's edge and catch that scent again.

The tour led us to a group of professors by the faculty housing. Our guide introduced us to two elderly witches who stopped to shake hands with the kids while other professors merely offered a lift of their chin. Faculty members were easily identifiable by the burgundy sweater most of them wore.

The tour guide addressed us, hands clasped. "The beauty of Shadowvale is that one does not need to be a witch or warlock to teach or attend. As long as they have the knowledge and qualifications of their respective subject, they're welcome here. Like Professor Bell and Professor Holden here. And over there is Doctor Leek, our Physics professor who was studying the motion of matter through the protection spell's magic. Though they do not wield magic of their own, their knowledge of its interaction with our world is vast. Some of the best teachers are those who are not tempted to practice magic because they can study it without distraction."

My mouth fell open as I gaped at each one of them. I never considered those of us without magic could teach at a place like Shadowvale. Not that I had any knowledge of how magic related to the natural world.

Two human teachers smiled and nodded. One wore a quintessential tweed coat, and the other donned the burgundy sweater with the embroidered "S" over the heart. The guy in tweed nearly blinded me with his smile. Sunlight glinted off a silver tooth, shooting a bolt of searing pain through my head. I looked away, focusing on the obvious shifter woman who waved hello from afar. Like I had wolf ears, she had orange and black ears that framed her high auburn bun.

Finally, we arrived at the best part of the tour. The cherry on top of the sundae, the climax of the movie, the piece of popcorn with the most butter. The library where they'd studied and stored *The Book of Prophecies*. Towering before us was a gothic building that could house this entire campus and most of Bewitcher's Beach. More gargoyle statues, like those on the Main Hall, perched high above us. Except these were not identical—nor still.

One of the gargoyles caught me staring at his muscular wings, and he cracked a side smile. My cheeks burned at the reminder of Sett. Like these gargoyles, the sheriff back home watched over me. It made my blood boil as much as I appreciated it. The way Sett tried to tell me what to do was inappropriate at best. He wasn't my bodyguard and didn't need to be, especially now that I was unofficially seeing a handsome reaper. Though that was as casual as my jean jacket and wrinkled Van Halen T-shirt.

I averted my gaze and hurried inside. A stained glass ceiling curved in the vast space above us. Bookshelves three times the size I'd ever seen before lined the round room. Indoor plants of every kind imaginable sat on desks in the center, beside plush velvet chairs and between sections of shelving.

When Doctor Leek came into the library, I slipped away from the crowd to speak with her. Just for a moment. The kids busied themselves gawking at the thousands of books anyway, especially my son, Jovi. He pushed up his glasses so he could fix his eyes on a grimoire titled *Becoming a Banshee: A Spell to Experience Spirithood* while the others poked and peeked at books in the familiars section.

Maybe I didn't understand physics, and maybe Doctor Leek knew nothing about the prophecies in the grimoire, but it was worth a chat in case she had any idea where *The Book of Prophecies* went. I sidled up to her as she dropped a tower of books on the librarian's desk.

Doctor Leek doubled back when she turned around. Maybe I stood a little too close.

"Hi," I said, beaming like a kid at the candy wall in Mockbuster. She arched an eyebrow so I stepped back and gave her an awkward little apology wave. "You're the physics professor who was studying the protection spell, right?" She nodded slowly, eyeing me up and down. I took another step back out of her personal bubble. "I was, uh, just wondering if you had any idea what might have happened to *The Book of Prophecies*."

She sighed, blowing an unsettling mix of odors. Ammonia, burnt toast, and rotten fish. I bit my bottom lip to avoid gagging at the smells of fear, regret, and guilt mingling in one icky swirl. Did she feel this about...the grimoire? The spell? "I wish I could say I had any clue where it was. I was about to make a breakthrough."

"Do you think it was lost accidentally? Or taken?"

She only forced a smile. "I have to run. I'm lecturing on the other side of campus in fifteen minutes. Maybe talk to Madam Rowena about it, she oversaw the protection spell study and—"

she glanced at her watch— "she should be in her office all morning."

I opened my mouth to ask if we could chat again, but she side-stepped and marched for the doors. My heart sank, but it didn't stay in the pit of my stomach for too long.

The tour guide announced that we only had one more stop before we enjoyed a late lunch in the cafeteria, where the field trip would conclude.

We exited out of the back of the library to find a row of smaller, more modern buildings. I gaped at the lecture halls as we trailed alongside them like a parade of small-town super-naturals.

We quickly cut through one of the classrooms, where the tour guide introduced us to an elementals class. Students painted symbols on their palms to siphon energy from the elements: heat from a candle's flame, cold from an ice cube. The kids lost interest when the tour guide explained that the purpose of the siphoning was to reduce the impact on the environment from air conditioners and heaters. They listened again when she segued from siphoning from the elements to siphoning magic from animal familiars.

At the end of the row of classrooms, the tour guide stopped and pointed to the last building. "Before we enter, we must go over a few rules. This is where all of the animal familiars are housed when they are not with their bonded person. They come here to relax, so please only pet those who approach you and do not stick fingers into any huts!"

We shuffled inside. An array of chirps, barking, meowing, and even croaking greeted us.

Hundreds of huts large enough to house the biggest familiar filled the room. They looked like dog houses, which made sense for the first familiar I saw. A wolf. The arctic wolf stared at me with white eyes from where she lay with her paws crossed at the front of the cushion. A single floating light glowed above her.

Even the smallest animals had the same size hut. Each creature enjoyed a unique layout in their hut depending on what they preferred. Huts housing rodents were designed with tubes and tunnels for them to hide in. A bat hung upside down in a bare hut without a light. Birds flitted about in open-topped huts with bars for them to perch on.

"Welcome," a man's voice boomed. I broke eye contact with a particularly grumpy armadillo. The creature glared at me before burrowing into the heap of soil at the center of his hut. When I straightened, I zeroed in on the source of the voice. The tour guide introduced the tweed-clad human as Professor Holden. "I am the familiars professor, and this is one of my students, Ted. He's here to work on his senior spell, and even though he's not a familiars expert, you can still ask him questions, and he'll do his best to answer." Ted gave the class a cheerful wave as the professor continued. "Today, you get to meet some of the most powerful familiars in the West. The—"

A tiny hand shot into the air. "Does the wolf bite?"

Another hand went up before he could even answer the first question. "Can I take one of the toads home? You have four of them and I don't think you need them all."

All at once they flooded him with questions, like a water breaking loose from a dam in a movie about natural disasters.

"Do you have any Axolotls?"

"What's an Axolotl?"

"I want a Guinea pig."

We chaperones shushed the kids, but it was nine against thirty-five and none of us came prepared with a whistle. Why didn't we bring a whistle?

"Mr. Holds Them!" A young witch jumped up and down. "Aren't those Coach Dean's familiars?" She said, butchering the dean's nickname. She pointed a finger at a group of odd animals all sharing one hut. They appeared bonded with one another. A black widow perched between a fox's ears. The other fox licked its paw, and a vulture sat at the top of the hut, watching over all three of them. They didn't look as comfortable or at-home as the other familiars.

Professor Holden nodded and opened his mouth when someone squealed and said, "The vulture wants to eat me!"

"Excuse me, Mr. Holds Them," my son shouted in a brief silence. "Why are you the familiars teacher when you can't even bond with one?"

The entire room fell silent. Oof. My skin prickled. Dio must have been paying attention when the tour guide said Professor Holden didn't have magic. As a human, he'd have to have a witch or warlock in his lineage. Even then, it might be so weak he likely wouldn't be able to wield it.

My skin prickled as Professor Holden's sharp green eyes landed on my son. Did Dio offend him? Pepperminty curiosity filled the air and blocked my ability to sense any smells from the professor. His frown said enough until he quickly flipped it, flashing a wide grin with a few rapid blinks. "Well, that's a great question. Familiars don't typically bond with someone who doesn't have magic, but it's still possible."

The kids were listening now, attention as rapt as mine. My eyes glued to Professor Holden as he stepped to the side and scooped the armadillo from his burrow. Clumped dirt fell off of the professor's hand as he held the angry little bugger up for everyone to see.

"Brick here is small, but his capacity for magic is as big as a water tank. Animals with magic simply boost a person's natural abilities. If you're inclined to sing well, for example, a single touch of Brick's shell might help you hit notes you've never reached before. That is, if he was trained by you or bonded with you. Otherwise, touching his shell would just be giving him a bumpy pet."

Nearly every pint-sized hand shot up but none of them shouted out this time. They were interested enough to be patient now.

The tour continued as we shuffled forward to admire the twenty-five cats in each of their huts. Once we exited out the back, I caught my daughter with a tiny, glittering hummingbird perched on the tip of her finger. The little creature took flight for a moment, buzzing wildly before it landed back on her finger and twittered.

"Stevie," I whisper-shouted. "Stevie!" She didn't turn around. The rest of the students and chaperones focused on an ostrich and emu that Professor Holden beckoned to the edge of the pen. I squeezed through the crowd and tapped her shoulder.

Stevie ignored me, still chatting away with the tiny bird. "Why? Are they bad guys?"

"Stevie!" She finally twisted, staring up at me with wide, unblinking eyes. "What are you doing?"

"Flit's talking to me."

I chewed on the inside of my cheek. I didn't want to reprimand my daughter for her natural talents. She seemed to understand animals in a way that nobody else did. If that was another tie to our potential witch ancestry, I didn't want to tamp it down. Could she be bonding with this little— "Wait. Flit? Did you name him that?" I sighed. "Stevie, this isn't a Disney movie, and you're not Pocahontas."

She shrugged. "Flit told me some of the people here are like evil villains. They're inventing something bad."

My pulse skipped. Was her drama the result of watching too many Disney movies or did the hummingbird actually share information? I glanced at the tour guide and then to the professor and his students.

I eyed them. They definitely didn't look evil, with their plaid scarves and cozy sweaters. But Doctor Leek? She'd smelled suspicious. And the gargoyle outside the library unsettled me. Maybe Flit was talking about them or even a student. My best bet was to ask everyone, not a professor, student, or faculty member spared.

I stepped up to Professor Holden, who'd broken free from the kids. "Mr. Holds Them—" I cleared my throat. "I mean, Professor, can I ask you something?"

He gave me a deadpan stare. "You just did."

I forced a smile, unsure if he was joking. "I'm the person who uncovered *The Book of Prophecies*. I was just wondering, since I know all the professors had a chance to look at it, do you have an idea where it may have gone?"

He released a weird laugh. "Me? I'm just the glorified poop scooper. I don't go near the grimoires."

A nasty sour odor sloughed off of him. Ammonia. Fear. Maybe he was lying and was worried someone would figure out he'd lost the grimoire. Maybe it was as simple as the plain fact that the horse pen was piled high with poop. He hadn't done any scooping in a long time.

Why did all the professors around here smell so suspicious? I needed to talk to Madam Rowena as soon as yesterday.

CHAPTER 4
THE INVISIBLE DEAN

WITH BELLIES full of pumpkin and porridge, we trailed single-file out of the cafeteria and into the center of the Main Hall. The tour guide stood at the landing between two sweeping staircases that followed the curve of the circular room. The second story housed more faculty offices but was open to the high ceiling rather than a narrow hallway. A black chandelier the size of my kitchen suspended in the center above us.

The tour guide bid us goodbye as we showered her with gratitude. When she turned to ascend the stairs, children buzzed with the excitement of their future and how they'd someday apply to attend Shadowvale. Others argued about whether a worm or a camel would be a better familiar.

Hattie returned to us as scheduled. She floated toward me, her golden dress rippling with beauty against the glow of the flames from the chandelier's candles. I updated her on the smell of the professors' lies and my plan to talk with Madam Rowena and the dean before we left.

"Noema," Hattie said, voice sharp but quiet. The thick Hollywood lashes that hung heavy above her eyes dipped as she surged closer to me and dropped her voice to a near whisper. "My friend told me that the dean is missing. You won't be able to talk to Coach. She vanished at the same time *The Book of Prophecies* did."

"WHAT?" My voice bounced off the ceiling, catching in the dome shape and echoing back at us. The tour guide froze at the top of the left staircase, her hand on the banister. Even Halen and Dio stopped fighting long enough to look at me. I swallowed my shock and forced my voice ten notches lower in volume. "Why didn't we know about that? The dean missing is huge news."

Hattie gave me a grim smile. "The school is keeping it quiet so students and parents don't wig out." Her gaze crawled over me. "Case in point."

"Do they think she took the grimoire? Is there a missing persons investigation on her? I have so many questions."

Another chaperone shouted for the children to line up single-file based on their grades. All four of my kids hopped into the third grade line.

I floated over to them in a trance and gave them each a crushing hug. Hattie lingered at my heels, knowing I was saying goodbye because we wouldn't be leaving with the group. I cupped Stevie's face in my hands and looked at them all. "Remember how I planned to stay here longer to study the spell book?" They nodded. "Grandmae will be picking you up when you get back to the school."

They loved that idea. Dio pumped a fist into the air as Halen did a little jig and Jovi grinned. Stevie shrieked and grabbed Halen's shoulders to shake him as hard as possible. After giving them each one more hug, I slipped into the hallway with Hattie.

Ghosts watched us from inside the walls, some hiding inside the portraits while others carried their chill alongside us.

Whenever they paused long enough, a bit of frost spread over the wall or ground where they stood. This extreme chill wasn't their only difference from Hattie, but I didn't have time to compare apparitions and oranges.

I marched to Madam Rowena's office with a million questions buzzing in my brain. The quest for answers burned like adrenaline in my blood. Taking a slow breath, I forced myself to calm before raising my hand to knock at her door.

Nothing.

I hit my knuckles against it harder.

Nothing.

"Hello?" I knocked again. "Madam Rowena? It's Noema Wolf." My ears perked at the sound of papers shuffling. I caught the faint scent of smoke, but there was no fire or heat that I could feel. Madam Rowena was behind that door, and that smell meant she was irritated. Hattie and I exchanged a glance, and I gave her a slight nod to confirm what I assumed she was thinking. Yes, I smelled Madam Rowena and yes, she was blatantly ignoring us. Hattie could have phased through the wall, but polite ghosts didn't invade people's privacy.

The odor shifted from angry to the icky stench of fish left out to rot in the sun...guilt. What was with all the faculty around here? Guilty, hiding, dodging questions. Something was horribly wrong, and it wasn't just the dean's disappearance with the grimoire.

If Coach stole it, would they ever find her? My legs itched to run. To wolf out and land on all fours for a race through the forest. To follow that smell.

Patience, Noema. Madam Rowena, the chief academic officer, would have the most information. Not only did her job work side-by-side with the dean's position, but Madam Rowena oversaw the study of the protection spell. She had to have a lead. I forced myself to keep my feet in place and knock again.

I counted the seconds into minutes, my foot tapping with each second that passed. Finally, the doorknob twisted and the door swung inward. Madam Rowena stood at the threshold, mouth in a flat line. Other than the arch of her brow, she was the picture of sophistication, like a painting of a famous witch with sleek dark hair pulled into a tight bun and body clad in a pale lavender pantsuit. Shoulder pads completed the outfit with a puffed up, superior style.

"You want to know where the grimoire is," she said. It wasn't a question.

"Do you know—"

"No," she snapped. "Do you think I'd have these dark circles under my eyes if I did?" Leaning out the door, she checked both sides of the hallway and then lowered her voice. "This is very deep, Noema. You have no idea what's behind that question. The grimoire isn't just missing."

"So is the dean," I said, finishing for her.

Her mouth twitched, but her lips still looked perfect in plum lipstick. "It is so much more than that."

"What do you mean?"

Madam Rowena rubbed a shaking hand over her forehead. She shook her head and fixed her eyes on the floor between me and Hattie. "We have to find that book."

"What about the dean?"

Her head snapped up, and she glared at me. "Obviously her too." But the same icky smell I traced in Doctor Leek and Professor Holden trickled from Madam Rowena too. Guilt, guilt, guilt. So much fishy, stinky, rotten guilt. What had they all done? A phone suddenly blared from the desk behind her, and Madam Rowena lurched. Without another word, she slammed the door in our faces.

"That's it," Hattie said, her voice laced with as much irritation as I'd smelled on Madam Rowena. "I'm going to Jane to ask her what she knows about all these faculty members." She wagged her wispy finger. "As the eyes and ears of this school, she listens. She knows. Plus, she's not just a ghost, she's a banshee. If you know what I mean." I only blinked at her until she continued. "A banshee? She loves to wail a good warning to anyone who will hear it."

I offered her only a half-hearted nod. "Tell me everything you learn."

"'Duh.' Isn't that what kids these days say?" With that, Hattie disappeared, leaving behind a chill in her wake. Maybe the ghosts here weren't so different. Just icier.

I waited to listen in on the phone call, but it was muffled and too slow. Madam Rowena barely said anything, and my entire body ached to do something. Something like taking another whiff of the familiar scent I caught by the forest.

ABANDONING MADAM ROWENA'S DOOR, I ducked through the halls. My limbs itched to drop to all fours because, as a wolf, I was faster and my sense of smell was keener. But shifting came with its downsides too. As a wolf, I struggled to form words, and changing my shape stole most of my energy.

Ghosts drifted in and out of the wall beside me, whispering unintelligible words. How much had they seen? I wanted to ask, but every time I looked directly at them, they'd vanish. Those were the tricks around here: vanish or stink like guilt.

Once I made it to the gardens outside, I bolted for the trees. Twigs and crispy leaves snapped beneath my feet. Despite the breeze, the heat of anticipation surged through my veins.

At the edge of campus and into the forest, I threw my head

back and drew in a deep breath. The hint of cinnamon sugar and rose perfume had grown fainter, buried beneath the smell of damp soil and tree bark. I tossed a look back at Shadowvale before dropping to all fours. The transformation happened in a blink, leaving my legs wobbling. My clothes floated to the forest floor, where I'd leave them until I shifted back to my human self.

The grimoire's smell caught my wolf's nose, stronger and powerful enough to follow. Carefully, I put a paw forward, not wanting to lose the trail. One step at a time, I tracked the scent.

Darkness blanketed me the deeper I drew into the forest. Thick trees blocked my view of the already murky sky. My heart pounded whenever the trail thinned. The scent was waning, whether from the breeze or because it had moved farther away, I didn't know.

The trail stopped cold. When I took a step back and dropped my head to the ground, I recovered the smell, however dull. I pawed at the dirt where the trail ended. It was freshly packed soil, like a shovel had just unearthed it, filled in a hole, and then smoothed it as flat as possible. A burst of the scent filled my nose so I pawed at the dirt again, tossing the damp soil between my hind legs.

The scent grew stronger with every scoop of dirt. I dug and dug and dug until dirt coated the fur on my paws and rain dripped through the concentrated cover of trees, pattering the forest floor in uneven drops. Finally, my paw hit something solid.

I bubbled with an excited bark and dug faster until I'd entirely uncovered an old trunk that looked like it belonged on the Titanic. Not in the ground by Shadowvale. Shaking with equal exhaustion and excitement, I gnawed at the clasp on the trunk. It came loose after a few bites and I nosed the top open.

It didn't give until I put all my force into it and popped a seal. The trunk exhaled with a hiss as I shoved the top open.

A horrible odor assaulted me, overpowering any remaining scent of the grimoire. Despite the stench, I hopped up, placing my front paws on the edge of the trunk, and peered into the darkness. My sharp eyes traced the edges of the contents piled inside.

Bones.

A human skull.

Waves of dizziness sent images tossing around in my mind. I dropped my paws back to solid ground before shock and sickness toppled me. I'd dug up the strangest coffin, and my brain was short-circuiting at the sight of someone's remains. Why did I scent the grimoire here? In this...grave?

I pawed at my nose and sneezed, trying to rid myself of the smell of decay before it haunted me.

A gust of wind swept through the trees, and something fluttered beneath the corner of the trunk. Or the coffin. Or whatever it was. I dipped my head and sniffed at it, scratching away the remaining dirt. Whiffs of rose perfume and cinnamon sugar eased my unsettled stomach at the same time it shot another dose of excited adrenaline through me.

Despite my wet fur, I was warm all over.

I pawed at the scrap of paper until I recognized that it was a piece of *The Book of Prophecies*. The first clue.

CHAPTER 5
BAD TO THE BONE

I GENTLY BIT DOWN ON the scrap of paper and tugged it from beneath the trunk. This piece of the grimoire was as precious as an available video tape of a new release on a Friday night. I pawed it from the stickiness of my mouth and pinned it to the dirt. The corner revealed a glimpse of *The Book of Prophecies*.

The scrap of paper showed two sketches with notes in the margins. I knew those drawings well. They were summoning shapes—circles which were meant to bring forth another being, and diamonds meant to trap their target in case of threat..

Summoning.

But why was a piece of this spell here? At a grave? Not even the most powerful witch could summon someone who had passed on. Ghosts were immune to summoning as far as I understood. Even if the target of their summoning was a lingering spirit, they couldn't be summoned. Someone had just reburied this trunk, and whoever that someone was, they also had possession of *The Book of Prophecies*. A spell like this didn't make sense next to a person's remains. Unless a ghost was the one doing the summoning. I didn't know much about

Shadowvale University's dean, but I knew she'd died mysteriously all those years ago. If these were her bones, maybe her spirit in the here and now was targeting someone who contributed to her death. Now that I'd experienced a slice of Shadowvale, I understood that it was an unspoken agreement around here to sweep secrets into the shadows. I snorted at the implication of the university's name.

The puzzle still didn't fit. Why would the dean return to her remains if she was summoning someone else? I padded to the trunk as I resisted the urge to gag. Hopping my front paws up to the edge, I peered inside. The odor had waned thanks to the breeze cutting through the trees.

Now that decay was swept away, a new smell replaced it. Unique traces of leather, of fermentation, and of cloves

The bones rested on a wrinkled burgundy cloth. The same shade of burgundy worn by the faculty at Shadowvale. Gently, I pawed the bones aside and thrust my head into the trunk to clamp down on the cloth. I tugged it from where it was buried beneath the skull. Laying it out in the dirt, I confirmed this matched the sweaters worn by everyone who worked here. I dipped my head, taking a sniff of the fabric. The scratchy wool tickled at my nose as I brushed it over the sweater and soaked in a familiar scent. It wasn't just the wool I recognized, but the combination of smells.

I knew this scent. I closed my eyes and breathed deeply, trying to dredge a memory from a lifetime ago. According to what Jovi had read from a science book at Bewitcher's Beach's library, smell was the strongest sense for evoking memories.

A woman appeared in my mind's eye. Tall and thin. Perhaps too thin, as though stress had taken a toll. A vulture perched on her shoulder, and at her heels stood two foxes. She cupped a wiry black widow in the palm of her hand. The sight of the spider sent chills trickling across my back. I finally focused on her face.

The dean. This was the witch in the painting. I barked with the excitement of another piece fitting to the puzzle.

She turned as if hearing a voice. The vulture took flight as another figure marched toward her.

"Noema, stop this!" she shouted. In the here and now, all the fur raised from my scruff to my tail. My ears shot back and tail tucked. I couldn't breathe as the memory filled in clearer and clearer.

This couldn't be me because the young woman didn't have wolf ears. Or it was before I turned...

Sour bile sloshed in the pit of my stomach. A whimper escaped me as I recalled what I'd done next. We were standing at the edge of campus, the woods at our backs. I lunged at her, planting the heels of my palms against her shoulders and shoving her to the ground.

Her voice echoed in my memory with a haunting cry.

"Don't do this."

The rest of the memory was faded, unreachable, as if I'd blacked out. The grimoire had sparked memories from before I was a wolf, but nothing else had ever done that for me before. Not until this interesting mix of smells. What was different now? Was my sense growing stronger? A sudden thrill lifted my heart for a moment before it plunged back to the depths of swirling bile.

I'd attacked the dean. She died mysteriously.

Then I came to Shadowvale decades later, and she ran.

She ran from me.

Her killer.

NO, no, no. This wasn't possible. I didn't have it in me to squash an ant, much less kill a person. I even hated accidentally stepping on a flower or uprooting a weed. I was a mother who sniffed out crimes to keep my family and town safe; I didn't commit them.

I shook out my ears and stepped back from the sweater.

"Noema?" A sharp, pitchy voice sliced through the silence of the forest at dusk. My breath snagged in my throat, and I tilted my head back. Hattie hovered at the edge of the hole I'd dug. Concern wrinkled her brow where a glittery headband wrapped around her head. "I saw your clothes at the edge of the forest. I thought you'd be running around like a wolf in here."

I sucked in fresh air and tried to form a word around my wolf tongue. "Wait," I said, managing to create most of the sound. After retrieving my clothes and using the last of my energy to shift back, I discreetly dressed myself and returned to where Hattie floated over the grave.

She stared down into the trunk, grimacing at the bones. "Mmm," she hummed without looking at me. "You certainly have a knack for finding suspicious things."

That was when the floodgates broke. I spilled everything, sharing with her what I remembered, what I smelled, what I suspected about myself. To my relief, she refused to believe I killed anybody, insisting that the memory was not proof of anything. Did I remember killing the dean? No, I only remembered pushing her.

With her confidence in me, I gathered the courage to walk back to Shadowvale and get help. She found a receptionist to call the police while I paced the hallway. After an indeterminate amount of time passed in a haze of pacing, I found myself back outside in the trees with Hattie and a growing crowd.

Before I knew it, police swarmed the forest.

Students, teachers, even Madam Rowena crowded the border between the Shadowvale grounds and the redwoods beyond. Police picked through the weeds and brush, flashlights sweeping across the forest floor where trees blocked the remnants of orange sunlight. Two other cops interviewed faculty, scribbling furiously on their notepads.

"Noema!" Senna shoved past two rubbernecking guys and threw her body weight into a hug. When she allowed me to breathe again, she glanced at the forest. Half of her many long braids cascaded over her shoulder. She wore a yellow plaid skirt and matching blazer that popped on her dewy brown skin. The outfit was a near replica of the clothes from the movie *Clueless*.

"This is the freakiest thing, isn't it?" She turned back to me, dark eyes swimming with the worry that matched the smell sloughing off of her. Anxiety, unease, and fear all smelled of ammonia. The stinging odor hovered the crowd of onlookers and mingled with a dash of curiosity's peppermint. She glanced at her palm, where ink in the shape of a flower was smudged. She cursed and craned her neck to look at my back. "I got a little siphoning ink on your shirt, sorry. I was at elementals class when everyone decided to ditch early and see what was up with the cops here. I wish I'd siphoned more heat from the fireplace before coming outside." She ran her un-inked palm up and down one arm to warm up. It didn't work. Her teeth still chattered like a skeleton in a Halloween decoration.

I squinted at the police trudging through the forest. One stopped and pointed at the ground while another hurried over with a shovel. Behind them, a woman in uniform hefted something heavy out of the ground, shifting it into another cop's hands. When the beam of a flashlight swept over it, I saw the trunk. "That's a lot of cops for one discovery." If I didn't know better, I'd think this was the set of a crime movie with the drama amplified. They must have already suspected murder.

Senna sucked in a long breath. "I heard rumors the dean died here a long time ago but her body was never found. So so freaky. They never told the students this, but now we're all finding out. I only knew because my ex-boyfriend's mom works at the police station. Now the cops are questioning everyone." She twisted one of her braids around her finger, tugging and tightening it until her skin strained from the squeeze. "It was crazy. The chief of police yelled at me as if I was the one who murdered somebody."

I followed her line of sight to a man with two chins and a Super Mario Brothers mustache. He even wore white gloves like Mario. With a huff, he hefted his blue jeans closer to his belly and then crouched, eyeing the trunk. A fierce frown twisted his face, and his gaze flicked to me. Stunning golden eyes stared me down, and knowing passed between us. Two werewolves sensing one another's presence.

"They've located the remains, so why are they still walking around?"

Senna's brow furrowed, eyes wide and unblinking at me. "Because all of the bones from the victim's right hand are missing."

Without breaking his gaze, the chief of police reached for the radio attached to his pants. He pulled the coiling wire from his belt and spoke into it. My ears shifted forward, alert and able to catch bits and pieces of his conversation. "I recognize the wolf woman's scent...bring her over here."

What? Me? Unease sloshed in my stomach.

A female cop stepped up from behind me. She gripped my elbow and instructed me to follow her.

I twisted, craning my neck to speak with the cop marching at my heels. "I'm just here for a field trip and I wanted to help find *The Book of Prophecies*." She said nothing. Her silence only sent my heart skipping. That and everyone watching me like I was some kind of criminal. My voice pitched higher as awkwardness spilled out of me. "Do you want me to help? I can help by shifting to my wolf form and trying to catch a scent for the hand bones. But that's only if you want—" My rambling cut short when she came to a sudden stop and grabbed my arm before I walked right into the chief of police. "Hi?" I squeaked.

He rubbed his mustache and drew a sharp breath. "I'm Officer Harbour. I'd like to ask you a few questions." He waved lazily, gesturing at faculty and students lined up in front of another officer. "I trust you'll cooperate like everyone else." A curt exhale blew through his nose and he folded his arms. "Have we met before?"

This wasn't the question I expected. Crime scene interviews usually started with a general identity of the witnesses. *Tell us what happened. Did you see anyone?*

"I live in Bewitcher's Beach, hours away from here, and it was my first time visiting a couple weeks ago. So, I don't think so?"

"I *do* think so, but you say you've never attended Shadow-vale?" His eyes narrowed, and the smoky hint of fury rose around him. What could he possibly have to be angry about? I shook my head and brushed hair off my neck. My curls were out of control from the forest's humidity. Strands stuck to my skin left sweaty from stress. "Interesting." It was all he said before he reached for the radio and twisted away from me to speak into it. "What kind of DNA?"

The radio buzzed with static before a female voice responded. "Hair or fur. At the bottom of the trunk."

He turned to me again. "Miss, I have a keen sense of smell

that provides aid during investigations such as these. That being said, I recognized your scent immediately and that it matches pheromones at the crime scene."

"Oh, yes, I dug this up when I was following the smell of the missing grimoire." How long did my scent linger? Could he detect that I was only at the scene of the crime for mere moments?

Seeming to understand this, he nodded and continued with routine questions. He filled out an interview sheet on his clipboard. With the break, the tension in my muscles melted away and I realized afternoon had dipped into evening.

The crowd dwindled as other officers dismissed students and faculty. Officer Harbour looked up and dove into another round of questions, hounding me as if I were a main suspect. I spotted Senna out of the corner of my eye, a look of worry on her face as she left with the other students.

Another officer interrupted the interview. The woman who'd dug out the trunk addressed Officer Harbour. "We're unable to locate the rest of the skeleton. We cannot find the hand bones."

"Does the medical examiner have an estimate on when the victim died?"

The woman swallowed and worried at her lip for a moment before giving a faint, curt nod. "Approximately twenty years ago. Maybe more. Likely a female, mid-forties."

"It's her," he breathed. "I'm sure of it." A sudden blast of wet earth—the damp scent of rain on soil—filled my nose. I glanced between the woman and Officer Harbour. The thick stormy smell of sadness was strongest near him. Was it from disappointment in his team?

After a hard swallow, he jutted his chin toward the forest. "Keep looking."

"Sir, we've searched everywhere and—"

"Keep looking," he growled, and the officer shrank away. His golden eyes raked over me before they flicked to the clip-board, then back to me. Finally, he sighed and mumbled a generic form of gratitude for taking the time to speak with him. He turned and marched off, effectively freeing me. But guilt still caged me. The memory of my fight with the dean was like walls closing in on my mind.

I hurried to find Senna and Hattie before exhaustion left me collapsed on the forest floor. It was a miracle I'd even managed to shift back to my human form. Now all I wanted was a hot meal and a bed for tonight.

Thanks to Senna sharing her dorm room and meal card, food and a bed was exactly what I got. I couldn't leave Shadow-vale now. The missing grimoire was almost enough to stay before, and now solving this murder pushed me over the edge.

I could almost hear Sett telling me not to involve myself in criminal investigations. But what Sett didn't know was that I might have been a key part of this case from the moment it began.

CHAPTER 6
PARTY PRATTLE

AN HOUR later I sank into the flat mattress in Senna's dorm room and reached for a turquoise phone. Hattie had disappeared to spend time with Jane, and I relished a moment of silence, until I plucked the phone from the receiver and dialed the number for Mockbuster.

After I informed both Grandmae and my pack of pups that I'd be home from the trip in a few days, I punched in Sett's number and lay back on the bed.

The line trilled and trilled.

Both Senna and her roommate were gone for the evening, studying in the library. As much as I'd wanted to join them and catch bits of information spreading through gossip, I was wiped. Not even a Diet Pepsi splashed with a bit of whiskey would revive me now—the whiskey being Senna's idea.

The ringing continued, but the call never made it to Sett's answering machine. Either he was on the other line and ignoring the call or the machine was disconnected. Maybe he was still at the station. I propped up on my elbow and dialed Bewitcher's Beach Police Department.

The trilling became an endless buzz in my ear as I scanned

the dorm room. An array of posters decorated the walls with boy bands and singers leaning against one another and staring directly into my soul. A clunky black boombox filled the top of the dresser that split the two twin beds into separate spaces. Two thick binders full of CDs sat atop it. I didn't have to look to know that the music inside matched the posters depicting the Spice Girls, the Foo Fighters, and Yellowcard.

As if on cue, blasting music filled the dorm. Senna's room-mate swung the door open and gave me a little wave, mouthing "party time" in my general direction. I dialed the police depart-ment another time, praying he'd answer. The beat of the song drowned out the ringing on the other line. I watched as Alicia dug a six pack of Heineken beers from under her bed. The blonde witch danced back out into the hall, the green bottles clinking against one another with every swing of her hips.

"Hello?" Sett finally answered, his voice scratchy and tired.

"It's Noema. I'm still at Shadowvale," I said quickly, before he questioned why Backstreet Boys was booming loud enough to destroy my hearing.

After a momentary pause, I heard the cluck of his tongue. "Did you get involved—"

"Okay yeah, maybe I interfered. But it wasn't my fault!" *Don't you dare say I told you so.* He chuckled, and I pictured him shaking his head. A whiff of smoky irritation rose around me until I remembered why I'd called him. "I'm serious."

"And you called just to confess?" Amusement still danced in his voice, and it was just like Sett to be entertained by my exasperation. Of course he'd crack a smile when I wasn't there to see it. He was probably happy to have me out of his way to work on whatever the heck he worked on when there were no investigations.

"Hey, you were the one who didn't want me to leave. Maybe I called just so you wouldn't have to miss me any longer." *Okay, rein it in Noema.* I called with a question and for help, not to argue with a grumpy cop for the second time today. But a little bickering felt good. I found an odd comfort in our teasing along with the familiarity of his response.

"You know what I miss?" he asked. "I missed out on renting *Contact.*" Bette didn't keep the shop open as late as me, and Sett likely didn't wrap up at the station in time to make it over to Mockbuster before she'd locked up. "I could be listening to Jodie Foster communicate with aliens while I tag all this evidence." Evidence? My lungs tightened and my mouth went dry. Before I could speak, he anticipated the question buzzing in my chest. "It's a shoplifting case at Chanel's Boutique. Nobody died."

Sweet relief flooded my lungs with fresh air. I sucked in another breath. "That's where you're wrong. Somebody did die." I dove into the explanation head first, confessing my impatience at trailing the scent and finding the bones. I told him everything up to the point where the werewolf chief of police said he caught my scent by the remains. Well, everything except my new memory of shoving the dean.

The song switched from pop to rap, and a cheer erupted from the hallway. Laughter followed until the students started chanting for someone to take a shot of liquor. I folded my wolf ears back, tuning out the party. "So about my scent? Can I really be blamed just because he smelled me at the crime scene?"

"I told you not to interfere—"

I bristled. "That's not an answer. And I didn't just interfere, I helped. Because of me, we now have a clue on where the grimoire went. Or at least where it has been. So instead of lecturing me about what I can't change now, tell me what I'm up against."

He released a long sigh. "Your scent was at the crime scene

huh? The legality of that is complicated. It wouldn't hold up in court. My guess is he will want to talk to you again. Just to get a better understanding about why your scent lingered there."

"That's outrageous!" I was desperate, wishing I could forget the memory of hurting Coach all over again. Now I just wanted reassurance. *Tell me I'm safe.* "So let's say I stumble upon a body..."

"Which you have."

"Right, and let's say it happened outside of Bewitcher's Beach. Let's say the police don't know I'm innocent like you do; am I a goner? Arrested? A major suspect?" He muttered but I didn't catch it. I paused, waiting for him to repeat it. "What was that?"

"You're innocent of killing, but you're not innocent, Noema."

"Excuse me?" I snapped. Staying angry at him felt better than allowing fear to creep in.

He released another sigh. I swear I could smell judgment dripping off of him in the scent of burnt toothpaste. It was an annoying combination of anger and curiosity. "You went and got involved. You did exactly what I said not to."

"So? It's not like I'm your employee and you're my boss." I sounded like an indignant teenager. Embarrassment burned my cheeks, but the shame melted as quickly as it came. Sett had no clue what it was like to know nothing about yourself. I may have gotten involved, but *The Book of Prophecies* was the only way to find my family. If these bones were tied to the grimoire, I couldn't just ignore them.

"Noema, I worry about you because I just want to keep you safe."

"Well you're not my bodyguard either." Memory of the gargoyles outside the grand library flashed in my mind's eye. The arrogant smirk on the guy's face only stirred the boiling pot in my belly. Before I shouted out like someone half my age, I drew a calming breath. "I called you for help. Not a lecture."

"I'm sorry. Listen, all you need to do is cooperate and you'll be home before you know it." Not that I wanted to leave yet. Not until I found *The Book of Prophecies.* "You'll have to answer a few questions. They'll grab your alibi—"

"Wait! My alibi?" A pit opened in my gut and I squeezed my eyes shut, pinching the bridge of my nose with my free hand. Hearing it spoken aloud gave it a sense of reality I hadn't attached to it yet.

"What about it?"

"I just thought of something. What if—" I swallowed. "What if I was involved and I can't remember my alibi from back then? They said the bones are a decade old."

"Then Officer Harbour will just have to dig deeper until he gets answers. Werewolves have been framed before." His voice softened, and I almost felt it wrap around me like a hug. Or like the inviting smell of his fresh sourdough loaves. I wrinkled my nose as the burning scent of cheap alcohol stung. Someone must have spilled it in the hallway. The students chanted for another drunk victim to take more shots of liquor. "Don't worry, Noema. If you need me, I'll only be a phone call away. I'll reach out to Officer Harbour and let him know you've ah... helped with investigations here. That way he knows your scent was at the crime scene because you're used to consulting."

I gripped the phone as if I could give him a hug through the line. "Thank you."

"Any time. I've got your back."

The smell of key lime pie, citrus, and a dash of vanilla mixed and drowned out the sting of stale tequila. My hope and happiness and the feeling of being loved embraced me with an array of delicious scents. *I've got your back.* Once upon a time, he referred to me as his backup, and he'd never failed to be mine. My lips parted, but before I could say goodbye, Alicia burst into the room and grabbed the phone, tugging it out of my hands. Behind her, Ted, Senna, and another guy I didn't know piled into the room.

"You're partying with us tonight," Alicia said. She jammed the phone on the receiver and shoved a bottle of tequila in my hand. Behind her, Senna mouthed *sorry*, but the smirk on her lips betrayed her. The sloppy giddiness of liquor had already gotten to her. She leaned against Ted.

Alicia screamed at someone in the hall to shut off their music. When the tune disappeared, she popped a CD into the boombox and grabbed the handle, hefting the bulky black device along with her to the hallway. It blared with a tune from Boyz II Men.

Before I knew it, I was wading through a party swarming with sweaty students and beer kegs. They'd transformed the student lounge downstairs into a temporary nightclub. Every curtain was drawn to block out any witnesses, but the music was cranked loud enough to wake the dead.

After half an hour, I found myself in a horribly uncomfortable bean bag chair while Hattie danced and laughed with the partygoers, clearly enjoying this callback to her days as a drunken flapper girl. She only occasionally paused to see if I'd had any success scouring for a lead.

I leaned forward, attempting not to tip my Diet Pepsi. "Aren't you worried Madam Rowena or someone else will hear this?"

Alicia, who was sitting with one leg draped over Ted, shook her head. "Nope!" she said, beaming and running her fingers through her pin-straight blonde hair. "I cast a soundproof charm. And if Madam Rowena or Coach asks, I'll just tell them it's experimentation to support the hypothesis for my senior spell."

Senna took a swig of her pale beer and then plopped into the bean bag that butted up against mine. "I don't know why she thinks that'll work. Alicia's project is about tying spirits to physical matter, not soundproof charms." She leaned against me, stinking of wheat and whiskey as she drunkenly whispered, "But I swear the charm's use is intended for good. We kind of all do that with our school projects. Ted's working on a spell with Professor Holden that confines wayward spirits, so we fashioned the confinement ingredients for sound."

"Ugh! Can we talk about how Professor H is literally so annoying?" Alicia drawled. "I hate that every time I want to visit Ted between classes, I have to see Professor H. He's literally obsessed with animal familiars and he always reeks of cat piss—oh my goddess, I'm going to puke."

Senna ignored her and continued, "Just don't tell Madam Rowena about any of this. She'd suspend us so fast."

The new guy scoffed. He tossed an empty beer bottle at a trash can, but it missed and the bottle clattered to the carpet, rolling and spilling the last bits of fruity beer on the rug. Alicia shoved him, clearly flirting with both Ted and him simultaneously. "Care to share your thoughts with the class, Teddy?"

Ted gave her a drunken, lazy smile and then panned his gaze to us. With a shrug, he scooted to the edge of the stained couch and leaned his elbows on his knees. He rubbed his hands together like he was warming them over a bonfire. "You know the dead chick from like eighteen years ago?"

"You mean the bones we found three hours ago?" I asked, trying to temper my impatience with their drunken antics. If Officer Harbour didn't consider me suspicious, I'd let loose and enjoy a few beers too.

Ted snapped his fingers and winked at me. "That's the one. My mom's a coroner. She told me to prepare my senior spell to present only in front of Madam Rowena, not Coach. Because the bones..." He paused, holding us all in suspense, though I could guess what came next. "They're Coach's."

Alicia tossed her head back and laughed. "Ted, you're such an idiot! That can't be right." She gave him a weak punch in the bicep, her red solo cup splashing a fizzy clear liquid on his gray flannel. Why didn't she believe him? Of course she couldn't smell the lavender whiff of truth that drifted from him, but the timeline fit. "Coach has been a ghost for like—"

"Two decades," I said. Of course, I already knew what they were just working out. Those remains belonged to the dean of Shadowvale. Sobering, Senna sat as straight as a beer-pong table and we exchanged a knowing look, likely realizing Coach's death had gone from mysterious to a murder investigation. Ghosts couldn't remember details of traumatic deaths. And speaking of ghosts, Hattie surged toward us at the sound of Alicia's squealing. Her transparent eyes flickered over us as she listened to Ted.

"Right again," he said as he threw his hands behind his head. He interlaced his fingers and leaned back, slouching into the cushion, head casually propped in his palms. "So my mom said Coach died in September of 1980. Now, eighteen years later, her bones are found, and it's at the same time her spirit goes missing? Freaking wild." He spoke conspiratorially, as if we were young children in a bad supernatural film. "Anyway, my mom says bones don't fully decay until the ghost passes on, but now Coach's tether is missing too, " he said, referring to the object that tied ghosts to the mortal world.

"Freaking wild," Alicia parroted.

"Anyway, Officer Harbour's going to ream whoever took his wife's tether."

"His *wife*?" I asked.

Ted tilted his chin back. "Yeah, Coach is Officer Harbour's wife."

Now that was something I didn't already know. The sadness I'd smelled on the chief of police made sense. Officer Harbour was simultaneously investigating both his wife's death and her missing person's case.

Did she take her tether and *The Book of Prophecies?* Or did someone else steal the tether, effectively kidnapping Coach? If she was kidnapped, it was possible her kidnapper was also her killer. Maybe I was in the clear. I definitely didn't steal the tether or the grimoire. It also made sense a killer-turned-kidnapper would want to swipe the grimoire before the protection spell was tested at Shadowvale, effectively blocking all intent to harm. If we found Coach's tether, we'd find her, which would uncover proof that I didn't kill her. Unless she *did* take them both and ran when she heard I was visiting Shadowvale.

I winced.

I bit my lip and shifted my attention to Ted, who looked half asleep now with heavy eyes. "Do you know what kind of object Coach haunted?"

He laughed, and his brows curved with skepticism. "She's called Coach for a reason." I glanced between the students, who smelled of burnt toothpaste. I sneezed and then shrugged, awaiting Ted's explanation. "She was the best freestyle footbag player in Shadowvale history. She haunts a *footbag*." A footbag? Like the crocheted ball of sand the students tossed around in the courtyard? Between that and the woven protection spell, I was becoming more convinced witches crocheted as much as they cast magic. "She used to keep it on display in her office."

"Ugh," Alicia said. "That room is a hoarder's hellhole. Coach keeps everything. Literally records and crap dating all the way back to when Shadowvale was established. Her entire office reeks like an antique store."

Her office. Tomorrow, I'd start there.

I'd caught a scent on Coach's Shadowvale administration

sweater; maybe I could try to catch the scent of her footbag and follow it right to her. Maybe the scent lingered in her office where she'd shelved the tether. If that didn't work, I hoped the smell of her office might jog another memory or three.

At the very least, maybe I'd figure out what the heck I was doing on Shadowvale's campus all those years ago. If Coach kept decades-old records, I might even find a file of my own.

CHAPTER 7
SPIRITED ACCUSATIONS

THE REST of the party was a blur of pop music until minor magic went awry. After last night, I understood the poster I'd seen pasted on the cafeteria wall. *Don't drink and hex.* Illumination charms had caught the curtains on fire, and when an extinguishing spell aimed to put it out, we ended up coated everyone with crystalized baking soda that left us itchy and covered in blooming rashes.

Senna and I squished atop the small mattress, but whiskey and sleep deprivation sent her into dreamland with no problem. She snored while I lay awake, scratching and scratching. Endless itching forced me to roll out of Senna's bed at the break of dawn.

All I wanted was a breath of fresh air away from the alcohol-stained rugs and humid haze of too many bodies crammed into the tiny dorm. A morning walk would do me good before I snuck off to Coach's office. Maybe I'd get a chance to talk with Madam Rowena and smell for more clues before a busy day swept her away.

Though I'd only allowed Senna to splash a drop of whiskey

into my soda, my temples still pulsed with pressure. The stress hangover eased with a gulp of crisp morning air.

Outside the dorm building, I soaked in the smell of toasted cinnamon drifting from the cafeteria and a distant hint of redwood bark. Cool air soothed the itching, and all urge to scratch my arms faded. Leaves crunched beneath my boots as I marched past the faculty building, sights set on the library.

I waved to two familiar professors, the woman with fox ears and the man wearing a tweed jacket and a crossbody bag. The bag hung heavy against his neck, weighed down with thick books. As he approached, I recognized Professor Holden and Doctor Leek. They offered me a meager smile as we passed each other.

A shadow crossed overhead, and I squinted at a gargoyle swooping above. He landed by the corner of the library and sent a miniature quake rippling through the ground, then his gaze panned to the professors.

"Professors, you're out early," the gargoyle said, greeting them.

"The ghosts were wailing something awful all night," Doctor Leek said. "There was no use trying to sleep."

I never heard them, but Alicia had cranked the music so loud I wouldn't have heard anything over the Spice Girls singing "Wannabe."

Professor Holden stopped to push his glasses up his nose and heft the bag's strap from his neck to his shoulder. When he spoke, his tooth caught the morning light and left my vision temporarily streaked with jagged lines. "Jane's brigade have taken to taunting and terrifying again." His voice dropped to an unfriendly tone at the mention of Hattie's friend. I slowed and angled my wolf ears to catch the conversation behind me.

"Are the ghosts bothering you?" the gargoyle asked.

As discreetly as possible, I swiveled to aim my nose in their general direction. One of them released fumes mixed with the smells of fear and irritation. Burnt cat pee. Yuck. Even worse than burnt toothpaste. The ammonia stench waned, but the crinkle of Holden's brow revealed he was scared of the ghosts. "Just Jane and her clique. They've gone wild over this cold case."

The gargoyle folded his arms with a scrape of stone against stone. "Is that so? Are you afraid of a few ghosts, Holden? Isn't that what you have that ridiculous silver tooth for? Because the ghosts have never liked you all that much?" He seemed to stifle a chuckle. It was rude, but I couldn't disagree that the tooth looked a bit odd. It was oversized and shaped to a sharp point as if the professor was pretending to be a vampire.

"It only protects me if they try to attack me. It doesn't stop harassment. They're blaming the faculty for what happened to Coach." Professor Holden blew out a breath and switched the bag's strap to his other shoulder. "Tell them to get off our backs."

"Respectfully, that's not my job," the gargoyle said. He expanded his wings, stretching the Shadowvale T-shirt tightly against his back as he took flight. He landed above us, perched on the edge of the library's roof to survey the school.

They gave up on the gargoyle and walked away, disappearing in the faculty housing. When the weight of the gargoyle's gaze fell on me, I forced a smile and then hurried to the Main Hall.

The massive oak door groaned as I dragged it open. The sconces that flickered with dim golden light weren't enough to illuminate the dark hall. When the door eased shut behind me, I was grateful for the clouded morning light streaming through the windows and casting a peachy hue across the floor and walls. I followed the curve, keenly aware of my clunky footfalls in the echoing hall.

Framed witches and warlocks watched me. Painted eyes shifted with my every step. Ghosts floated from painting to painting, some trailing me while others stopped to whisper, making it appear as though the painting's mouths moved along with the eyes. My wolf ears perked to catch their hollow voices.

"Where is this wolf going?"

"Isn't that Jane's friend?"

"Friend of a friend."

I almost stopped to introduce myself until memory of the professors' fear prodded me to walk faster. Jane was likely friendly, but the taunting they mentioned made me think the rest of these ghosts weren't.

"Murderer..."

My blood chilled. What did they just say? I spun around to face the paintings, but the artwork was flat and lifeless. No one was there. They weren't talking about me, right? If only I could hear who they accused.

"Do you know something the police should know?" I asked. My voice bounced off the wall, falling flat in the empty space.

"Murderer."

I picked up the pace, nearly jogging to where the hall branched off into four narrow hallways. In every side hall, each door had a plaque with the faculty member's name etched on it. I darted down the second hall, but the voices echoed here too.

"Murderer!"

With my heart in my throat, I grabbed the handle and wrenched, trying to push through Coach's office door, but when I stepped forward, I flopped against the door. It didn't budge. I twisted the handle again but it was no use. The office was locked up tight.

Chewing my cheek, I decided to move on. Impatience had me nearly jogging back down the hall to Madam Rowena's office. If I could get her to talk, could I convince her to unlock Coach's office for me? Not likely, but everything was worth at least one try.

Rounding the corner, I spotted Madam Rowena's door. I raised my hand to knock when a face appeared in the knotted wood. Two transparent eyes filled the triangle in the A's on the plaque that spelled MADAM ROWENA. I slapped my palm to my mouth.

"She's not here," the ghost said. "Gone. All of them, gone."

I mustered my voice. "Where?"

"To the police. They had to answer lots of questions. Especially Madam Rowena."

"And the professor." Another ghost joined, though I couldn't pinpoint where this one was hiding. "Both dark, dark pasts."

Why were they speaking so cryptically? "What do you mean?"

"Both arrested once."

Oh, that was nothing. I'd been arrested. So had Hattie, back when frequenting speakeasies was a crime. Still, curiosity's peppermint permeated the surrounding air. What once put Madam Rowena in jail? And were they speaking of the professors too?

I opened my mouth to ask the ghosts if they knew more, but the walls seemed to move as they fluttered in and out of the wallpaper, the door, the paintings. They disappeared in a flurry as a voice echoed through the long hallway.

Someone was humming—coming closer and closer. Claws extended from my fingernails, and my teeth grew into canine fangs. Just in case whoever scared the ghosts was truly dangerous.

A flash of gold rounded the corner. Hattie surged down the

hallway toward me. "Noema, do you hear what the ghosts are saying?"

"That I'm—"

"Shh!" She shoved her wispy finger through my lips. The chill left my teeth aching as if I'd just bitten into a popsicle. "Don't give them more reason." Her voice dropped. "We need to figure this out before the rumors get wild. As soon as the fuzz confirmed this was a murder, the ghosts went a little nuts with the news. Excuse my French, but they're *dying* to find their precious Coach. Jane believes Coach's spirit still exists. She swears she'd know if Coach passed to the afterlife. Do you have any ideas on how to find her and solve this?"

I chewed on my lip and nodded. "Yeah, but you'll have to break me into the dean's office. Are you cool with that?"

Hattie smirked. "I've broken into the safe of a bank and then evaded the fuzz. All in one night. What do you think?"

I suppressed a smile at the gutsy flapper girl who had been defying the law since before I was born. Maybe all I needed was a whiff of that office to remember more. If I could collect enough memories, I could collect an alibi. Maybe an end to this whole nightmare was in sight, and like Sett said, I'd be home before I knew it.

CHAPTER 8
[REDACTED]

HATTIE NAVIGATED the shifting hallways like a racecar driver. The ghosts trailed us in a whoosh of whispering conversations. They phased in and out of the walls, sending me into a dizzy spell as they appeared in the crown molding, and then in front of us, but never long enough to ask what else they knew. It was as if they wanted to be involved but refused to help.

Hattie vanished through the door to Coach's office, and the other ghosts no longer swirled around me. I waited impatiently, dancing from one foot to the other like I needed to use the restroom.

I shoved my sleeve up my forearm to check the Swiss Army watch wrapped around my wrist.

Finally, the latch clicked. Hattie had solidified her ghostly form enough to turn the lock. I grabbed the doorknob and twisted, slipping through as quickly and quietly as possible. After closing the door, I spun around and scanned the office. Hattie surged toward the bookshelves at the opposite wall, humming about Coach's tether as she went.

A curved window cast rays of blue and purple light across a

massive desk. The desktop had rough edges and an odd shape to keep the image of the tree it was cut from. A magenta crystal ball sat beside a clunky desktop computer that looked out of place next to the dark furniture and heavy indigo curtains. Two towering bookshelves packed with hundreds of books, crystals, glass wands, photo frames, and folders flanked the window. Apothecary cabinets lined the side walls, likely storing files or spell ingredients among their dozens of drawers. One was smaller than the other to fit alongside the wall with a black door.

I closed my eyes and drew a deep breath, trying to pinpoint the smell from Coach's Shadowvale sweater. Nothing smelled of fermentation, but I caught the scent of cloves and other herbs along with a hint of leather. Trailing the natural spices, I shuffled to the smaller of the two apothecary cabinets on the right next to a closet. I swung the door open to find a collection of faux fur and leather coats. That explained where the bit of leathered aroma came from. Leaning in, I identified notes of fermented cloves, but it wasn't strong.

I sniffed for a drawer where the spice of cloves came the strongest. Rosemary twigs filled every inch of space in the first drawer. I slid it back inside and tried the next drawer. More rosemary. The third drawer was full of mint, and the fourth smelled like Christmas pine before I even opened it. I dropped to a crouch and took a sniff, waiting to distinguish the different scents.

The smell drifted up from down low. The cloves were at the bottom of the cabinet. I shuffled through all the drawers until spotting the tiny brown sticks. Finding them was underwhelming. This didn't explain the combination of the smells that triggered the memory.

I sighed as I stood and hurried to Hattie's side. "Find anything?"

"If you count this shape in the dust as something." She pointed a finger at a round break in the dust that coated the middle shelf.

"I bet that's where her tether was."

Hattie was no longer looking at the evidence of the taken object. She eyed me. "Are you sure sniffing around in here will help you remember where you were when she died?"

"No, but it's all I have."

Turning to face the back of the desk, I caught the same combination of smells I'd scented from the sweater. My heart thumped, and I hurried to yank out the flat drawer above the chair.

An array of office supplies rolled back with the force of my pull. Pens, pencils, scissors, staples, paperclips, a lighter, and a worn box. Some of the other items didn't match, like dried biscuits in the shape of chickens and the empty exoskeletons of a bug that looked like a Cicada. I frowned and reached for the box. Sliding it open, I found the source of the smell. Leathered cloves and fermentation.

Coach must have smoked cigars. At least, she once did a long time ago when she was alive. It was common for ghosts to mimic many of the habits they enjoyed during life. Hattie "tasted" her favorite foods through their smells, and it seemed Coach may have done the same with these exotic spiced cigars. That explained why her coats vaguely carried the same smell while the sweater was soaked the strongest. She likely wore it the most.

I lifted the box to my nose and took a slow sniff. It dredged up the same memory of me attacking Coach. Her scent definitely triggered a real memory.

I shivered and shoved the cigars back into the drawer. This wasn't helping me recall anything new. I went through the other drawers but only found more evidence of her familiars.

Packs of dried meat for the vulture, half-chewed tennis balls for the foxes, and stainless steel bowls next to bottles of purified water.

Nothing smelled as strongly as Coach's cigars. Maybe the scent only triggered that specific memory because it was the only time I was around her long enough to smell her. Then why did I push her? What had made me so angry?

I edged around the desk and continued scanning for any clues of Coach's tether being taken, but the wall of photographs caught my eye. Dozens of photos decorated the wall. Some photographs were clearly very old, one even with Jane and five other Victorian-era witches. Over the years, the photographs became brighter, more colorful, and clearer. The witches and warlocks smiled at the camera. These orientation day photos must have been taken in the forties and fifties based on their bobby socks and poodle skirts. Later pictures showed students all standing in a similar pose. They held up their hands, palms out. Paint dripped from their hands and they stood in front of a stone in the gardens with hundreds of handprints. It appeared to be a tradition. The photos were in order, so I scanned down the line until a familiar face caught my eye in what looked like the nineteen eighties.

A very familiar face.

My mouth fell open and breath left my lungs. I was staring back at myself—my younger self just like in the memory. But this was so much clearer. This was real, a tangible photo. I stood between two witches and a shapeshifter guy with fox ears huddled at the far end. Like in the memory, I had no ears. No wolf ears, anyway. My dark, curly hair was draped over my shoulders, and I hugged a leatherbound book. Like the students and faculty, I wore a burgundy sweater with large brown buttons down the front. An embroidered insignia of a silver 3D "S" with a shadow behind it sat over the left breast.

Gingerly, I touched the glass on the frame as if I could pinch my younger self and prove to myself that this photograph was real, not a dream. "It's really me," I breathed.

My heart pounded, and heat flushed through my chest and stomach. The door to possibilities was thrown wide open, and it took everything within me not to shift into my wolf form and run up and down the hallways.

I'd come here for answers. Answers about my family and my identity. But I never expected to find out I was one of them...a Shadowvale student.

She looked so different and yet entirely the same. Younger me—non-wolf me. Was that why nobody could recognize me after I'd become a wolf? Was that how I'd lost track of my family? I had the same chocolate brown eyes and thick hair, the same curious, reckless, impatient look with a mischievous curl of my lip. But I never remembered seeing myself with the faint curve of high cheekbones or dainty, slight features. Either age or becoming a wolf had given me a stronger, bolder frame and facial structure.

Hattie stopped humming, and I suddenly missed the soothing tune of the old Vaudeville song. "Did you find anything?"

Oh I'd found something—exactly what I first hoped to find when I visited Shadowvale with the field trip. I opened my mouth, but now I couldn't find the words to speak. I had too many questions, too many emotions. Overwhelm swirled in my head like a tornado. Confusion, hope, joy, fear. Who was I? A witch? Was magic the reason I could smell emotions when other werewolves could not? Of course, all werewolves had a heightened sense of smell, some sensitive to particular things like illness within a person's body or junk food, like Dio. Why and how had I even turned into a werewolf? I'd buried such questions long ago, thinking I'd never really find the answers.

But this photograph was a gateway—maybe my own personal portal to half a lifetime lost. Did these other students know me? I wasn't standing with them, only caught in the photo's background, and even Hattie barely recognized younger me based on how I looked now. Hope that the other students would remember me waned. But I didn't need memories, I needed cold hard facts. Like records of my attendance at Shadowvale.

"Noema, are you okay?" Hattie surged to my side. Brows furrowed, she forced me to meet her gaze. "Did you get another memory of yourself at Shadowvale? You know that might mean you have traces of witch ancestry. But didn't your witch friend, Senna, already guess as much because of your mark?" With a glance and a curt nod, she indicated toward my collarbone, where the bat-like winged tattoo had appeared on my skin only months before.

"A witch," I said, still mumbling. I swallowed all the emotions, if only for a moment. "Something like that. Look." I nodded toward the wall of photographs. I moved closer to it, tucking my ears back as I sidled up against the apothecary cabinet. Cabinet knobs dug into my butt as I pressed myself as close to the picture as possible. I fixed a half smile onto my face to match my expression in the photograph. "It's me."

"Oh my word." Hattie hummed. "It's a little baby you."

"And before I was a werewolf." I took a long breath to calm the fluttering in my chest. A twinge at my temples threatened to return to full-blown pulsing. "I'm dying to know more."

"Well of course you are! If I didn't know my family or remember half my life, I'd be wigging out right now. I never would have recognized this as you without you standing right next to the picture."

If I was in this photo, I was definitely somewhere in Shadowvale's records. Should I ransack Coach's office on an emotional high? Definitely not. Could I breathe until I found my own student records and learned my last name or old address? No way. I struggled to take a full breath with all the butterflies buzzing in my chest.

I peeked into the apothecary, the drawers stuffed full of papers upon papers. Each one was carefully rolled into a miniature scroll. I pulled one out and unrolled it. Determining it was a student application and transcript, my heart flipped. This was it. I tugged every drawer open and shuffled through the scrolls as quickly as possible, scanning for names and dates.

Since I didn't know my last name, it was impossible to determine where my records might be—if they existed at all. It was a long shot, but one I had to take. A jolt of adrenaline rippled through me at the sight of the labels. Each drawer was split into sections with dividers that were labeled with dates. The first divider read *Fall 1998*.

"Oh wow, these are for students coming next year," I said. Each scroll was printed with the student's name on the outside and organized alphabetically by last name. I plucked a rolled paper from the middle of next fall's section and uncoiled it, quickly scanning an application for someone named *Morgana Steel*.

"Ninety-eight?" Hattie said. She peered over my shoulder for a moment and then, still solidified from unlocking the latch, she managed to unroll a few scrolls from the middle drawers. "Each drawer is about one school year. Oh wait, there're way less records and applications in the older years." She was at the bottom right, where the label read *Fall 1738*. The drawer was pulled all the way out, showing more dividers than I could count in a glance. In that single drawer, the labels spanned over one hundred years, proving her point about the lack of records in the university's beginning. But it also proved they stored records from centuries well before I would have attended.

After another minute of yanking out drawers, we found

four with labels between 1977 and 1981, when I likely would have attended. Since we only knew my first name, we scanned every document for that.

Thumbing through each scroll proved tedious, since these drawers included the students' transcripts, a copy of their diplomas, an essay from their senior spells, and their original applications. Not every student's scroll was packed with information. Some were merely an application and transcripts— from students who never completed their degrees, never achieved graduation, and never attempted a senior spell.

The clock ticked behind us as we shuffled through hundreds of papers in every drawer labeled 1980s, carefully replacing each one to their correct location.

Just when I thought the search was a lost cause, Hattie hummed an uplifting tune. I perked up at the look of her excitement and curiosity. Her eyes flew over the scroll that was unraveled and laid out on the top of the apothecary in front of her. "Noema, look," she said, voice low.

She pointed to the scroll with my first name and last initial. A black mark covered the rest of my last name. Beside the mark, a note read REDACTED.

Fire gushed through my veins, so hot it felt like the burn of ice. Was this really mine?

CHAPTER 9
REJECTED

SLOWLY AND WITH CARE, Hattie pinned back the curling edge of the scroll to reveal an application with my name on it. Noema T[Redacted] had applied for the fall of 1980.

"Why is your last name crossed out?" she asked.

I couldn't bear to look. Was this even me? I squeezed my eyes shut, slowing my panting breaths. Every emotion flushed through me, and I suddenly wanted to splash water on my face. Or maybe take a nap. Or eat something. Yes, I needed food after last night's late party. While I reeled, Hattie's eyes flicked over the application.

"What else does it say?" I asked, voice as squeaky as the chirps of my pet mouse.

"Let me read the short essay," she said. Clearing her throat, she quoted the words. "Applying to Shadowvale University is a lifelong goal to follow in my family's footsteps. I plan to study psychology and the effect of magic—"

"On emotional wellbeing," I said, finishing the sentence for her. I knew those words. I'd written those words. A distant memory flooded me with a vague image of my younger self. In a dreamlike blur, I saw myself sitting outside on a log near a lake, scribbling this essay on a scratch piece of paper while the application was neatly rolled and placed by my side. It wasn't only smells that triggered memories, but very specific words, like when I'd studied *The Book of Prophecies* and recalled glimpses of a life I didn't know.

"So this *is* you?" she asked.

My eyes shot open. Swallowing through a squeeze of emotions in my throat, I only nodded.

The longer she read, the more her lips twisted in concern. A line creased her brow and she hummed a faint string of curses in slang from the 1920s. Her reaction sent a wave of dizziness through me.

"What is it?" I asked, my voice scratchy and tight.

She sucked in a breath and pinned it open again. Heaviness tugged at her twisted frown. "Oh Doll, I hate to share bad news, but it looks like you didn't get in." She poked at the scroll to pinpoint a red rejection stamp and Coach's signature at the bottom. A neatly printed note filled the section titled "Office Use Only" at the very bottom.

I whispered it aloud to process the words. "Noema Redacted rejected on terms of violent offense. No!" My back went pin-straight and I grabbed the scroll, shaking my head as if the memory that confirmed this would fall out and be forgotten. "This can't be right. I'm not violent."

"What if it's not you?"

"It's me. I remember writing this," I said. Hattie hunched into a spiny slump while I shot to my feet. I paced back and forth across the office, white-knuckling the application. "What violent terms? One push couldn't be enough, right?"

Another frost chilled my veins and sent a block of ice to the pit of my stomach. I pinched the top of the scroll and unrolled it, checking for the date of the rejection notes.

September of 1980.

Terror gripped my throat, but I met Hattie's gaze and managed to squeeze out a single question. "Tell me you heard Ted say when Coach died."

"Yeah, 1980. September, I think."

My eyes fell shut, the darkness both disturbing and comforting at the same time. "That's the day of my rejection," I whispered.

"Doll." Her voice was sad, and she fell into the habit of humming a soft and haunting tune—her way of comforting me since I could barely feel her wispy fingers make circles against my back. The tune only lasted a few beats then drifted away to a tense silence.

My watch ticked the quiet minutes away until a voice echoed from the hallway. The harsh pitch drifted in from where the door was still open. Madam Rowena spoke in a clipped tone that matched her pointed footsteps. "I'm taking you to Coach's office while my receptionist looks for Noema. I can't promise we'll find her though. She isn't a student here. She's not even related to a student here." But I was almost a Shadowvale student. Once upon a time. "Did you call her hometown? She probably returned to Bewitcher's Beach."

"She's not there," Officer Harbour's voice responded.

Finally, my brain caught up with the situation. They were searching for me. The chief of police investigating a murder wanted to speak to *me*. And here I was rifling through the victim's office with my old rejection letter in my hand.

"Hide," I whispered. In a blink, Hattie vanished through the closed door of the closet. I hurried after her, opening the door as quietly as possible. I needed more information before the police interrogated me. I didn't have the memories to support an alibi, and I didn't know enough about my past self to determine if this rejection was a motive that pushed me to murder.

Inside, I shifted into my wolf form, dropping to all four paws. After nudging both my clothes and the rejected application into a dark corner, I nosed into the heap of fabric. I was larger as a wolf, but could easily bury in the mountain of shoes piled at the bottom of the closet and blend in with the fur coats that I knocked off the hangers. Most importantly, the faux fur coats should mask my scent in case Officer Harbour tracked me again. No crisp breeze here to carry it straight to him like in the forest.

Footsteps drew closer, and I hushed my panting, drawing my tongue into my mouth and sealing my snout shut. It was a hundred degrees beneath all that fur, but I was hidden and safe. For now.

Muffled conversation came from the other side of the closet door. It wasn't easy to make out their words until the footsteps drew closer. I'd tucked my ears as tightly against my skull as possible to keep from a furry tip poking out of the pile of shoes and fur coats, but I dared to perk one ear and catch Officer Harbour's words.

Light peeked in from under the door, only shadowed when a heavy footstep stomped by. I bit my lip and breathed as shallowly as possible. With every fall of the officer's clunky boots, my heart pounded harder and more erratically.

"And you said this office is usually locked?" Officer Harbour asked.

"Not *usually*," Madam Rowena said, a bite in her voice. "Always. This is impossible. The ghosts don't meddle around in here."

"Who has the keys to this room?"

"I do," she said. "As you well know, Coach is a ghost and prefers not to do the heavy lifting for things like keys."

"So it isn't impossible. Which sounds like you left a room

related to a crime scene wide open for anyone to disrupt." Officer Harbour met Madam Rowena's tone with curt words.

A moment of silence revealed the tension on the other side of the door. Beyond my own fear and worry and strained nerves, I caught the scent of irritation. Whether the hint of smoke came from Officer Harbour or Madam Rowena, I didn't know. Someone cleared their throat and then released a long breath.

Madam Rowena's heeled shoes clicked as she crossed the room, drawing closer to the closet and to where I estimated Officer Harbour was standing. "I'll choose not to take offense from your rude behavior because I know you're upset that Carissa's missing. But you cannot speak to me like that. Your wife entrusted me with these keys, and I have never misplaced them or left the office unlocked."

"Fine. Now what about Noema? Did you ever take her into this office?"

I bristled. He kept bringing me up. Did they have evidence that the past, violent version of me left behind?

A shiver twitched down my spine and all the way through my tail. It was impossible. I'd never so much as squashed a spider and I didn't have a temper problem. But patience? Thinking things through? I was still working on those. And maybe my impulse control was even worse as a young adult. Maybe I was reckless enough to retaliate against the witch who'd denied me entry to Shadowvale.

Emotions swelled and receded with a cacophony of smells. The stuffy space trapped every stench inside, thickening the air every time I tried to convince myself that past Noema was as innocent as present Noema.

"Not that I recall. But," Madam Rowena said, her voice cracking, "Noema is your primary suspect, correct? If not, she should be." Smokiness faded, and I wondered if the new smell came from her. I nearly gagged at the sudden rise of fish in the air. The rotten, icky odor like dead fish left to bake in the afternoon sun sloughed off of someone on the other side of the door. Bile pushed into my throat and tainted the back of my tongue with bitterness. Madam Rowena was blaming me too?

"She is, but I'd like to hear why you say that," he said. "You mentioned nothing of this when I interviewed you this morning."

She cleared her throat, and the sound of her clicking heels grew distant. I had to hold my breath to catch her words now. "Because now that you say it, I'm remembering *The Book of Prophecies* went missing at the same time as Coach, and Noema is even more obsessed with that grimoire than any witch." *Because it has a prophecy about me!* Madam Rowena knew that. She knew why I was interested in it. She was there when the strange mark formed on my collarbone. "And she called here regularly asking where the grimoire was, who studied it, and why Coach couldn't use her power to complete the protection spell." *Curses.* Madam Rowena was grossly exaggerating. I called twice to ask about the prophecy that mentioned me. I couldn't help my curiosity for my past.

"Noema told me that yesterday was the first time she'd been to Shadowvale," he grumbled.

"Absolutely not. She's visited before, just earlier this year actually."

That's not true! My stomach dropped. The dim closet went pitch black as my eyelids slid shut and I willed myself to stay quiet. As sick as the gross smell and deception made me, at least I knew the source of the guilty odor. Madam Rowena was lying through her teeth, and I swear it smelled like she had bits of fish stuck in her gums.

Officer Harbour scoffed. "And you failed to tell me this?

Madam, Carissa would be sorely disappointed in you, especially because you were someone she trusted."

"She'd understand," she said. "Carissa knows how stressful and busy it is to run this school. I can't remember every person that visits the campus. After you mentioned the timeline of Carissa's disappearance, it got me thinking."

Not only was Madam Rowena lying, she was shifting blame. Was she covering up her own crime? Or did she remember me from years before and only now put it together? My tail tucked tighter between my legs.

A heavy sigh came from one of them, likely Officer Harbour. "I can't say you're wrong about that. Carissa was so busy this last month that she opted to stay overnight on campus to get it all done. She never came home. The most I'd get was a phone call to tell me she was still alive—er, you know what I mean."

"Yes, we've all been busy with the new semester starting and the arrival of *The Book of Prophecies*."

Except the grimoire went missing before they could study much. Maybe Madam Rowena stole *The Book of Prophecies*, though I couldn't conjure a reason she'd want to do that when the best and brightest witches to perform those spells were right here.

Sadness filled the air with the scent of rain on soil as Officer Harbour spoke. "Truth is, I blame myself. I was so swamped at the station, I don't even know how long she's been missing. My own wife!"

"I'm sorry, Jet," Madam Rowena said. At least she didn't stink up the room with another bout of guilt. She truly was sorry. But was it for his grief or because she had something to hide?

"And you say she was locked away in her office, right? You're sure you didn't see her?"

"That's right. The last I heard directly from Carissa was a couple of days ago. That was when I received a message from her to lock up *The Book of Prophecies*. But it was already gone. I thought she was in deep study of the spells she had copied from it."

"That thing is the bane of my existence," he said. "She's obsessed with it."

"Yes, you're not the only one who thinks so. I overheard professors complaining that she's putting her heart and soul into it and therefore rarely available anymore."

Officer Harbour coughed and cleared his throat. "Anyway, while I'm here, I should look around, and then I'd like to talk to the teachers. Plus anybody that knew Noema. Hell, just plan to pull people to the cafeteria for interviews all day."

"Will do."

After a few more minutes of tromping around the office, their footsteps finally receded. I threw my head back, tossing off the suffocating furs. Desperate for air, I panted as quietly as I could, waiting and waiting and waiting.

For once, I was patient, waiting in the humid and suffocating closet because I couldn't let them find me. Not yet. Not until I dredged up more memories and recalled what I was doing the night Coach died.

Not killing her, hopefully.

CHAPTER 10
SUMMONING SODA

BY DUSK, I'd failed to conjure any more memories. Even the potent smells in the potions classroom did nothing. I tried taking a whiff of Madam Rowena's office while she was out, but that didn't help either. The only scent I caught was the smell of her familiar posted up in front of a filing cabinet. The wolf had growled at me, but since I'd given her a wide berth, she didn't howl any alarms or lunge at me. So, I poked around at Madam Rowena's desk long enough to find a letter signed by the dean.

A letter signing over her *role as dean* in the event that something happened to her.

Since this discovery, I couldn't think of anything else.

Though the document was old, dating back before Coach died two decades ago, it was well preserved, which meant it was important to Madam Rowena. If Madam Rowena wanted this role, I'd uncovered her motivation to kill Coach. And if she did kill Coach for this, it was possible her plan was thwarted when Coach's spirit lingered, allowing her to hold the title as dean even after becoming a ghost. Maybe Madam Rowena waited all these years for Coach's spirit to pass on to the afterlife, and when she didn't, Madam Rowena kidnapped her to finish the job and claim the title.

My plan to use memories to find my alibi fell away as I dove into research on Madam Rowena.

In the meantime, I became invisible. Well, as invisible as an almost six-foot-tall woman with werewolf ears could, and only to Officer Harbour and Madam Rowena. I'd ducked through the halls and used Hattie's help to stay out of sight. She'd phased through the walls to check each hallway and room for signs of those two before I dared set foot inside.

Now four hours later and in Alicia's borrowed clothes, I almost blended with the crowd of college kids. Almost. I didn't exactly fit in, but Senna and her friends knew how to party in the shadows, so I was well hidden here. With a dozen noise-cancelling spells, the guys' dormitories sounded as quiet as a study hall from the outside.

Hattie and I stood at one end of a plastic table in the dorm's downstairs lounge. Several red cups lined both ends in a pyramid shape. Beer filled each cup to the brim, sloshing over the sides when Ted bobbed a ping-pong ball into one. Alicia playfully cursed at him for making a mess while Senna sidled up between Hattie and me with two tiny glass cups full of vodka.

"This one's for you," she said in a singsong voice, nearly bumping into me as she offered me the shot glass.

I gave her a deadpan look. Maybe she was already two or five shots in because she only blinked at me cluelessly, forgetting why I couldn't risk inebriation. I'd told her I planned to chat with as many senior students as possible and find out what they knew about Madam Rowena. I had to understand why she'd lied about me. I had to know if she killed Coach all those years ago because that meant I didn't. It was a hopeful shot in the shadows. Much better than a shot of alcohol. "You said

Madam Rowena tests all the senior spells at the end of the year, right?" She nodded, eyes lazily dipping to the cups in her hand. "Do you know much about her?"

She squinted as if she didn't understand the question. Tilting her head side-to-side, she said, "I know she's a hardass. And I know that presenting the senior spells in front of her is so scary it once caused a warlock to die of a stress heart attack."

My jaw may as well have been the ping-pong ball bobbing into the cup of beer. Even Hattie flinched, her ghostly body flickering into a dull glow before returning to a clear form. Apparently, Madam Rowena was worse than a liar—she was truly terrifying. "That's horrific."

Senna gave a limp shrug of one shoulder. "Eh. It's not so bad. Apparently, the dude is un-living it up as a ghost. He went off to travel the world because his tether is a map. He built a teleportation spell but it didn't work when he presented it so he just...died."

"Can somebody on that side of the table throw the damn ball?" Alicia shouted. Ted switched off between both teams, throwing as both Senna's and Alicia's partner. Then he disappeared to do a keg stand with a group of rowdy guys.

I fished a ball out of a cup of water at the side of the table, cleaning off the sticky remains of beer. Lining it up carefully, I lofted it in a gentle arc so that it would drop straight into the front cup. It dipped into the cup in the row behind it. Ted shouldered past two people making out just in time to view my victory. Raising both hands, he whooped loudly and gave me a high five.

Alicia scoffed and rolled her eyes before resolving to pick up the scored beer and down it carefully enough not to spill on her pink Juicy Couture track suit. Smoky irritation rippled off of her and dissipated into the overwhelming scents of happiness and excitement. Different odors mingled in the fun too, from jealousy's body odor to sadness's earthy scent of rain. I glanced at a young witch in the corner who hugged her arms around her midsection and eyed a couple heavily kissing on the couch. Other than her, most students smiled and laughed.

"Nobody looks too stressed out here," I said, noting the entire lack of ammonia in the air. Not a soul at this party experienced enough fear for me to smell. You'd think a room packed with this many seniors would have at least one student overwhelmed with the biggest project of their life on the horizon. "How soon do you have to present the spells?"

"Four weeks. We're getting down to the wire." Senna replied. "Most of us have our spells completed and we're testing aspects of them. But we can't cast the whole thing until presentation day. It's wild, honestly. Like, if my decoy summoning items don't actually summon a ghost, I'm coming to live with you in Bewitcher's Beach. I'll get plastic surgery and change my name and nobody here will ever hear from me again." She sipped at the shot glass and scrunched her face before pointing it at me. "Hey, maybe I'll become a werewolf! Then I can forget about failing."

Okay, she was definitely tipsy. Senna would never be that insensitive when sober. Not that I hated being a werewolf. But forgetting half your life was not a fun little party trick. A thought surfaced like the ping-pong ball. Though it wasn't a memory, I formed a picture in my mind's eye. I saw myself in the burgundy sweater casting magic. What if I'd attempted a spell to convince Shadowvale faculty that I was worthy, failed at it, attacked Coach out of anger, then chose to become a werewolf to forget everything and put it all behind me? Where would Madam Rowena's lies fit into that theory? Maybe she believed me guilty, but why create false information? I shook my head and faced Senna, who tossed a braid over her shoulder. The bead at the bottom clinked with the dozen other braid beads. "Has Madam Rowena's behavior been any different since Coach and the grimoire went missing?"

Senna smirked. "Take a shot with me before I answer any more questions, Detective."

A ghostly laugh erupted, and I slid my narrowed eyes at Hattie. She grinned. "Good luck, *Detective*."

I groaned. "Do you have a Diet Pepsi I can chase it with?"

"Hold my beer," Senna said, shoving the shot glasses that were definitely not beer into my hands. The smell left my stomach sloshing, so I passed the glasses to Ted. Senna muttered something else under her breath, then with a snap of her fingers, a can of soda appeared on the table right in the middle of the pyramid. The beer cups fell to the side, spilling foamy golden liquid all over the table. Beer poured over the edges of the table in dripping waterfalls that smelled of wheat and barley. "Oops."

Alicia's arms shot into the air, and she did a little dance that looked far too provocative for being in public. "Party foul magic! I win."

"Ooh," Ted said, nudging Senna with his elbow. "Causing a party foul with magic means you have to try to cast the hardest spell you know while shotgunning a beer."

Senna groaned. "I'm going to end up breaking something."

"You already did," Alicia said. She pointed a manicured finger at the mess of beer cups.

"Hey, yo!" Ted shouted, raising both hands again as if that was his natural state of being. Hopping onto the beer pong table, he lifted one of the glasses to point it at Senna. "We got a party foul with magic over here. Y'all know what that means? Beer spell! Beer spell! Beer spell!"

Soon half the room joined in with Ted's chanting. They pumped fists into the air, eyes on Senna as she rolled her eyes and reluctantly took Ted's hand. He lifted her onto the table beside him, and they collided when he caught her from swaying so far she'd fall.

The chill of Hattie's body slithered over my right side as she leaned into me with her shoulder. Literally. I rubbed the cold from the back of my arm. "Well, you got out of taking that vodka shot, but I don't think you're getting any answers, Detective."

I straightened. "Hey, wait!" I shouted. "Wait a second."

"It's useless," Hattie said with a laugh. "They can't hear you."

This was a disaster. I needed a lead on Madam Rowena, and these students were my best bet. If they weren't getting so goofy with alcohol. It'd be a full twenty-four hours before the partygoers would be sober and awake enough to help me out. The chanting turned into cheering and thumping feet as Senna finally nodded and accepted her fate.

I growled, and climbed onto the table next to Senna. "Senna, before you get too drunk, please help. I need to know. Do you know if Madam Rowena wants to be dean of Shadow-vale someday?"

"If you want an answer, then you have to take a shot," she said, eyes twinkling with mischief. Ted laughed and spilled the vodka from the now half-empty glasses into one glass before holding it out to me. They were loving this—fully amused by their alcohol-soaked offer.

And I thought eight-year-olds were wild. Someday, I'd be the mother of four college students. Yikes. My heart clenched at the thought of them. I couldn't wait to give them each a wolf-hug when I got home. The sooner I figured this out, the sooner I'd get to see them.

I snagged the glass, lifted it to my lips, and threw it back in one gulp. The liquid burned all the way down my throat and into my chest. I cringed while everyone else whooped and shouted.

Senna yelled over the noise. "So down here in the dorms, we have a phrase for Madam Rowena. She's 'the killer of dreams and the nightmare dean' since she basically takes over most of Coach's job for herself. Does that tell you enough?"

In a daze, I nodded. That told me more than enough. It confirmed what I'd suspected about Madam Rowena's motivation for murder. She wanted Coach's title, and, based on the students' perspective of her, she was brutal enough to take it.

Ted released Senna and hopped off the table. Like a sudden and unexpected gentleman, he helped me climb down. Senna was the star of the show now.

"Hey." Ted cut through my thoughts. I frowned at him, expecting another shot glass shoved into my face. Instead, he offered a drunken grin. "If you want to know more about Madam Ro-Ro The Killer of Dreams, you gotta talk with Doctor Leek. They know each other pretty well. She's co-taught classes with Madam—" His voice was cut off by ear-splitting cheers.

Crouching on the table, Senna held a permanent marker in one hand and was puncturing the base of a beer can with her dorm room keys with the other. Beer spilled from the hole and into her mouth. Without looking down, she drew a circle next to her on the table and then scribbled crude images as fast as she could. The circle wasn't fully closed, though this looked purposeful. She stopped short with the marker and drew each picture almost exactly the same distance apart around the circle, leaving the open space empty.

"What's she doing?" I shouted, but Ted only glanced at me.

"Chug, chug, chug!" Everyone chanted.

The pictures at the edge of the circle were vaguely recognizable. A beehive. A honeycomb. And two different types of flowers. The chanting built louder and louder until it was just white noise. I folded my ears back to block the sound as best as I could.

Senna tilted her head back farther and farther. Once she downed the last of the beer, she slammed the empty can over the spot where the circle wasn't closed. The moment the can completed the circle, a live bumblebee appeared, hovering at the center of the circle.

The room erupted into screaming cheers. The bee landed on the table in the circle and crawled across to a puddle of spilled beer. After a moment of inspection, it flew up above Senna's head and then buzzed off.

When the shouting died down, Ted finally answered my question. "It's a piece of her senior spell. She was summoning." It made sense she'd take interest in summoning. Senna herself was once summoned back in Bewitcher's Beach. "The theory of her spell is that objects touched by the living being's body are not needed for summoning if the intention behind the purpose for summoning is strong enough." I nodded as he spoke, trying to process what this meant. From what I'd seen, personal objects were used to summon tangible beings only. This spell would break the barriers of only using summoning magic on living beings and with their belongings. The objects here weren't real, just messy drawings, and they still summoned the bumblebee.

Alicia came up and hung over Ted's shoulders. "Blah, blah, Senna, blah. What Ted's not telling you is that he's creating a kickass spell too. In the shape of a diamond."

Wiggling his shoulders to brush her off, he turned to her. "We're not supposed to talk about it after it's turned in." She made a pouty face that he promptly ignored as he swiveled back to face me. "Anyway, if Senna can prove this works, reapers will be able to summon spirits instead of having to track them down. Actually, she said the idea was inspired by your boyfriend."

My heart jumped. With the new memory and discovery of my record here at Shadowvale, I'd pushed Crow out of my mind. Did he encourage Senna to create this? Warmth spread across my chest. If Senna's spell worked, maybe we didn't have to be long-distance lovers. Not that we were lovers. He wasn't even my boyfriend, despite what Senna called him.

Still, I wished Crow was by my side when I needed him. Like Hattie, or Senna, or even...Sett often was.

The party raged on with a blur of games and erratic magic. I sank into a sofa and listened for more information passed among students like spit swapped through drunken kisses.

CHAPTER 11
HANGOVER HINT

AFTER DRINKING ONLY ONE SHOT, I was down for the count. After the party, I collapsed into Senna's bed, and Hattie—who didn't normally need sleep—decided to snooze in Alicia's bed while the girls drank in the guys' dorms all night.

The next morning, I woke with a faint throbbing through my skull. Echoes of "Do You Wanna Get Funky" by C+C Music Factory radiated with every throb. It was a wonder the kids didn't blast out the speakers of the boombox the way my brain was blasting out of my skull right now. Must be from dehydration. I'd only drunk a splash of vodka, but it was enough to do a werewolf in after a night without plenty of water to follow it up.

Morning had arrived in full swing, streaming dewy light through the single window over Alicia's bed. The digital clock on the dresser glowed with green numbers. At half past eight, it should have been brighter outside, but the perpetual clouds gave Shadowvale truth to its name.

I rolled out of bed and mumbled for Hattie to wake up. I couldn't exactly shake her body to wake her up, so my voice pitched higher and louder until her eyes fluttered and one split open.

She took one look at the clock. "Nope," she said, sealing her eye shut again.

"Hattie, I need your help. I have to get around campus without running into them." By now, I'd been avoiding Officer Harbour long enough that he'd probably try to arrest me just for acting so suspicious.

"Sorry Doll, that music rattled my brain last night. I'm done for."

Mention of the pounding boombox had me rubbing at my temples. I massaged my forehead even though it did nothing to soothe the throbbing. Water first. If hydration didn't work, this had to be a stress headache.

"Okay, you sleep. I'll go talk to the lady who knows Madam Rowena." Now that my head was clearer, I mulled over what Ted explained last night. If their senior spells summoned spirits, could Madam Rowena have used that to kidnap Coach? It was so far-fetched, and yet the possibility nagged at me.

I used Alicia's bed frame to pull myself to my feet. Smoothing the wrinkles out of the borrowed clothes, I marched for the door. The hinges creaked when I swung it open, and a blast of icy air swept past me.

Hattie surged into the hallway, her back facing me. She glanced over her shoulder and winked from beneath her glittery headband. "What's taking you so long?"

It took me twice as long as her to make it down the two flights of stairs. She phased through the wall to check the lawn and walkways before I dared step through the door. With the all-clear, I yanked the door open and followed her to the science buildings across campus.

Hiding behind bushes and ducking into the shadows felt as silly as it was necessary. I had no doubt Madam Rowena would turn me over to the cops the minute she spotted salt and pepper wolf ears and curly brown hair.

Getting to the science buildings was an adventure well worth it. We'd arrived before classes started, for Doctor Leek's students anyway. With Hattie's nod, I pushed through the classroom door and stepped into the only lecture hall on this side of campus. Most of the science buildings were small laboratories, but since Doctor Leek taught Physics in Magic, which was a popular class, she took precedence over the shared lecture space. At least that was what I'd overheard between two science majors at the party last night.

We entered at the top of the steps. The view from here felt like looking down at an indoor auditorium from the nosebleeds. The door fell shut behind us, sending a slam echoing throughout the domed space.

Doctor Leek sat with her chin perched on her fist in front of a desktop computer. Though she was at the bottom of the vast room, her fox ears perked at the sound and she snapped her head up. Ripping off her black-rimmed glasses, she squinted at us. "Class doesn't start until ten."

Maybe she should trade in the near-sighted glasses for multifocal lenses. Or maybe I blended in better than I'd thought. I slumped. As a mother raising a strong pack, I wanted to look like it—not a fresh-faced party kid.

I followed Hattie down dozens of steps between rows of desks. Hattie was certainly impatient today. Usually I'd be right alongside her, chomping at the bit for answers, but I'd tempered my rushed behavior while Hattie, who didn't have a chronic problem with impatience, went with the flow of however she felt that day.

Doctor Leek picked up her glasses and peered at us through them. "You're not students."

Not anymore. Once upon a time in a past far far away though...

"No, but I'm interested in their work," I said.

She set the glasses on the keyboard in front of her and eased back in her chair. Folding her arms, she stared up at me. "You're that werewolf who was asking me about *The Book of Prophecies.*"

"Yeah." I forced an apologetic smile for ambushing her a second time.

"I'm sorry for running off last time," she said with a sigh. I bit my lip to stay quiet and allow her to explain her apology. Hopefully the silence would prod the rest of it out of her. After a moment, she swallowed and continued. "I didn't want to think about what happened to the grimoire. I was still telling everyone I was about to make a breakthrough, and I didn't want them to think I took it for myself. It is no small feat to understand the interaction of matter through the space occupied by the protection spell." She said it with pride, and as if I'd understand what any of it meant.

I resisted the urge to outright ask if she'd lost the grimoire. "So you weren't close to a breakthrough?" If she was close to understanding the section she'd studied, how much did the other witches learn about the prophecy that mentioned me?

She hesitated, foot tapping beneath her chair. Hattie folded her arms, clearly getting more and more impatient with this whole investigation. Surprisingly enough, she didn't throw out any blunt opinions yet.

Doctor Leek finally relented, and the floral smell of truth sloughed off of her. "I thought I was making a breakthrough." She sucked in a quick breath. "Until after it disappeared. I went over my notes again and discovered I'd made a mathematical error. I wasn't as close to success as I'd led everyone to believe." That explained the smell of guilt and regret she'd emanated before.

I carefully eased the conversation to focus on Madam Rowena. After a few minutes, it became evident Doctor Leek had nothing useful to say about the chief academic officer. They were colleagues, and from what I gathered, Doctor Leek was too busy to pay attention to Madam Rowena's goals, behaviors, and reputation. All she confirmed was that Madam Rowena was a rule-follower. When the discussion waned, Hattie's chilly energy grew tenser.

"Blast it," Hattie said, throwing her hands up. Her patience had finally unraveled. *Here it comes...* The ghost in a flapper girl dress mimicked the action of slamming her hands on the teacher's desk and leaning over her with intimidation. "Do you know where *The Book of Prophecies* is?"

Doctor Leek furrowed her brow. "I wish I could say I did, but no, I have no idea." No stench of rotten fish or burnt toast or anything unpleasant came from her. Doctor Leek wasn't annoyed by Hattie's suggestion.

"Fair enough." Hattie glanced at me, and I gave her a quick nod to signal that Doctor Leek smelled of truth. "Do you have any idea what happened to the dean?"

Her face fell. "No, and I haven't the slightest clue why anyone would ever want to hurt her." A layer of wetness shone in her eyes before she blinked it away. "She was the kindest, most admirable woman I'd ever had the pleasure of working with." Cracks cut through her voice.

I drew in a long breath as my gaze fixed on the professor's face. Lavender mingled with the scent of her sadness. She still didn't stink, which was both frustrating and a relief. She couldn't help us track Coach, but she was also cleared as an accomplice. I had to admit, I hadn't considered her a suspect despite her closeness with Madam Rowena. I was too fixated on Rowena to look further. Thankfully, Hattie's blunt questioning made this conversation easier. Now that we got that out of the way, we could continue unraveling the threads that led to Madam Rowena. If only the truth smelled this distinctly on everyone, Hattie and I would be a team of unstoppable investigators with her demands and my nose.

The hints of grief in Doctor Leek's scent drew me back to the present.

I offered an apologetic smile for her loss. "There's a bit of good news. I have a few ideas about where to look for the grimoire, and I'm hopeful that will give us a lead we can bring to the investigators." It wasn't a lie, though the end goal was several steps away.

Determine Madam Rowena's involvement.

Figure out how the grimoire fits into all this.

Track her until she leads me to it.

"You do?" Doctor Leek's spine went straight. A dash of hope's delightful scent trickled from her.

"About the spells, though, I was wondering, could Senna James' spell actually be used to summon a ghost?"

Her thick eyebrows sank and her lips flattened as she processed this. "Senna's spell is incredibly complex and dependent on Alicia's spell. As of now, we're only able to summon solid matter. Alicia's spell works to tie the spirit to matter. In theory, if we carve the spirit's name into a piece of its original matter, the spirit will bind with the matter and it will move the spirit through time and space. Simple, right?" Not at all. I was barely hanging on to understanding. Thankfully, Doctor Leek behaved with a lot more patience now than when I'd first met her. "But since this magic is intended to help reapers and the reapers will not automatically have the original matter, that's where Senna's spell comes in. She's designed the magic to make it so that we don't have to access the original matter. We can instead manifest a decoy of the original matter using the ingredients of a classic summoning spell."

"Could the decoy be a drawing?" Hattie asked.

Doctor Leek tapped her nose and then pointed at Hattie. "Exactly. That's a crude form of it that we've tested on solid matter. People are a collection of memories and experiences and preferences trapped in a body. We create the decoy with those pieces of what makes that person unique."

"So say the reaper doesn't need a decoy because they have what you called original matter," I said, my mind going a million miles a second. "Is that their body?"

"Yes. A hair, a flake of skin, any DNA."

Or a hand. My pulse doubled, the blood rushing through the sensitive veins in my ears. I could barely hear my own thoughts.

Each one of Coach's bones were in the trunk except for the right hand bones. The kidnapper took her hand in order to take her. They didn't even need Senna's spell. But where did they take Coach? What had Madam Rowena done with her? And why hadn't she declared herself the dean yet? Maybe there was a statute of time before it was deemed appropriate and she didn't want to look suspicious.

I opened my mouth to thank Doctor Leek for her help, but a piece of this puzzle didn't fit right. "How does this help reapers? They'd still need to know several personal details about the person who passed to create the decoy matter, right?"

Doctor Leek suddenly slapped the desk. "That's what I said! But Professor Thompson said Lucy's senior spell will take care of that side of it. I'm too busy to advise more students, though, so I can't tell you the details of Lucy's spell."

"And couldn't the spirit just leave before the reaper gets a chance to guide them?" Hattie interjected. "Speaking as a ghost, I've been there and done that. When you first become a spirit, you're terrified and unwilling to listen to anyone."

"I believe Ted Moore's spell is designed to address that."

Understanding snapped into place like a dislocated shoulder pulled back into the socket. Ted was talking about a diamond last night. Summoning diamonds were used to trap people. I'd been one of those people, summoned and trapped by a murderer before. The memory left me prickled with goosebumps.

"We can ask Ted, if you're curious," Hattie said to me as if she could hear the wheels turning in my head. "I know I'm curious."

"No," Doctor Leek answered before I could tell Hattie I was already way ahead of her. We snapped our attention to the professor, who put her glasses back on and was peering at us. "Ted's spell is complete, and he turned it in almost a month ago, which means he is sworn to silence until presentation day. He can tell you about as much as I did, but the details will get him expelled. It'll be viewed as seeking outside help."

"What about Professor Holden?" I asked. "Can he share details?"

"If he wants to keep his job, he won't spill the secrets of a senior spell. Besides, the students have to complete the final portion of the spell's creation without their advisor's help. None of us will have access to the full spells until presentation day. The finished essays and spells should already be locked away in Madam Rowena's files."

My lips parted. I'd seen a well-protected filing cabinet in her office. "Are they stored in her office, by any chance?"

She arched an eyebrow. "Yes, and guarded by her familiar, so I don't suggest trying to sneak a peek."

I forced a smile along with a half-hearted nod. I didn't care about the spell itself. But if I could prove Madam Rowena had possession of a ghost trap at the same time I had the students share what they knew about Madam Rowena's motive to murder Coach, would it be enough to convince Officer Harbour to consider her the number one suspect?

A sweet smell filled the air around me. Hope lifted my heart with the scent of key lime pie. If Madam Rowena was truly the killer and kidnapper, I was in the clear.

I'd be able to take a deep breath again. I'd be able to dig into my past here at Shadowvale and learn about myself. And best of all, I'd be able to return home to my pups with a clean conscience and a heart full of hope.

First, I had to know if his spell was truly a ghost trap. I just had to get past her familiar—and I knew just the professor to teach me how.

CHAPTER 12
A FAMILIAR FAMILIAR

YOU'D THINK a ghost and a werewolf wouldn't have so much trouble sneaking across a campus full of supernatural people, but we barely made it to the animal familiar dormitories alive. Well, I barely made it there alive. It didn't help that our path around Shadowvale had been overrun with witches practicing defensive magic. And where there was defensive magic, there were teachers projecting offensive magic.

Students swarmed the gardens, throwing up invisible shields using the powers of intention and elemental manipulation. I could make out the shapes of some of the wind walls used as a barrier against bullets. The force of the wind slowed the bullet enough to drop it to the stone pathway before it hit the student.

While the brilliant witches and warlocks used magic as protection, I ducked behind statues and bided my time until the teachers had to reload. Shadowvale was getting wilder by the day, and it had nothing to do with parties.

The craziness yielded one good result. Senna was outside of class and accessible for a chat. We gathered behind the wind wall, where it was safe from the bullets.

"Once we have more evidence, we'd like to share the students' nickname for Madam Rowena with Officer Harbour," I explained. "Is it okay if we tell him that you were the student who told us?"

Senna grinned, flashing dazzling white teeth at both of us. "Definitely! Honestly, the detective probably already knows she's terrifying—who wouldn't, you know? But I'll be happy to tell him how the students see her if you need more proof."

I nodded. "Thank you. We'll give you some kind of signal, if we need you."

Senna could reveal Madam Rowena's motive for murder once we revealed her means to kidnap the ghost of the murdered woman. Then Officer Harbour would have no choice but to *fully* investigate her.

Twenty minutes later, we stepped through the doors of the familiar housing, and Hattie turned to me. "So, were the teachers shooting real guns at students?"

I nodded. "I think so."

"Not quite," Professor Holden said. Hattie and I exchanged a glance. Was the professor talking to us? He stood crouched in front of the armadillo's house, not looking at us. The creature nosed out from the base of the dirt piled inside and glared at him. Professor Holden snapped his fingers and beckoned the armadillo toward him. After a tense two seconds, it seemed an invisible leash snapped around the armadillo's neck, and the little guy crawled into the professor's arms. "The bullets are etched with a charm that will disintegrate it when it comes in contact with the magic cloaking the students. If their shields fail, the bullets will never hit them."

An unexpected smell sloughed off of him. The scent of his anger burned my nose with smoke tinged in gasoline. I didn't expect him to be mad as he spoke of the bullets, but the smell came suddenly and grew stronger through his explanation of the bullets and defensive magic.

"That's kind of amazing," I said with a forced smile. I still didn't fully grasp how the magic here all worked.

"It's old magic actually." He finally stood and faced us with the armadillo cupped in his arms. The smoky odor dissipated as a refreshing blast of sandalwood replaced it. Professor Holden went from inexplicably pissed off to confident faster than those bullets. He stroked a hand over the armadillo's back, whose anger also appeared pacified. In fact, the familiar looked exhausted as it melted into the professor's arms and slumped against his body. I never expected that fiery little creature to be so calm.

"Thanks for the correction," I said. "We aren't—"

"Students," he said. "Yeah, I remember you."

Shoot. This was more dangerous than sneaking past those bullets. Did Professor Holden know about Madam Rowena and Officer Harbour's hunt for me? Or did he just remember me from the field trip? Senna had said they didn't spread the news. If they had made that information public, students would definitely have gossiped about it. That didn't mean Professor Holden didn't get pulled into the investigation by Madam Rowena. Maybe she thought I'd seek his help regarding my daughter and then he'd turn me over to the authorities when I inevitably showed up here seeking answers. She knew Stevie claimed to communicate with animals.

"You're the mom with the girl who tried to steal my hummingbird," he said.

I swallowed the thick worry that clung to the back of my tongue. Hopefully that was all he knew about me. "Sorry about that. That's actually what I came here to ask about. My daughter is very keen on animals." How could I word this to ask about Madam Rowena's familiar? I paused, eyes falling to the canine house where the arctic wolf was curled up. "But she was terrified of that wolf." His brows lifted, and the scent of his curiosity propelled my lie. "She's never scared of any animal. Is there a way I could show her that the familiar isn't frightening? We might come back for another field trip, and I wouldn't want her having more nightmares." The lies were just building and building, and I couldn't even claim they were for a good cause. This was a selfish cause—solving the investigation to prove I was never a murderer. Of course I wanted to help find Coach... and the grimoire. Oops. Now it was back to a selfish motive.

"I'm not sure what you're asking," he said. The smell of confusion peaked. "This wolf isn't aggressive."

Not like Madam Rowena's wolf. I shifted from one foot to the other as if I could jar enough ideas for a lie. "Even if she's not, my daughter thought so. So for the sake of this, let's just say the wolf is dangerous. Could I offer the wolf a treat just long enough for my daughter to pet her or anything?"

A strange smile cut across his face. "If it were that easy, don't you think familiars would just flip to bond with whoever gave them the best food?"

"Seriously, Noema," Hattie said between her teeth.

I shrugged. "Okay, so there's nothing we could do to show her that the wolf won't hurt her? She's having awful night-mares." I clasped my hands in front of me to show him how desperately I wanted help. I wasn't above begging if it played a role in proving my innocence. And if I wasn't innocent, I'd never write roles and plays again, much less fulfill the promise I made to my late husband. Sadness and anticipation swirled in my gut at the thought. I swore I'd write a screenplay for Holly-wood one day, and everything my husband did supported my dream. Since his death, I'd all but given it up. Any attempt to write the screenplay was thwarted by a complete lack of ideas.

Professor Holden stopped stroking the armadillo, and the

creature rolled into an armored ball. He kept his palm cupped over the armadillo's back. "There's only one way, and that's to bond with the familiar." I deflated. My back curved into a slump as disappointment set in. How could I find out if Ted's spell was a ghost trap? I couldn't turn Officer Harbour's attention to Madam Rowena without it, and I wasn't willing to risk approaching him on a guess. Maybe it'd be easier to get Ted to spill the spell's beans.

No. It sickened me to think of risking his college career for my own selfish gain.

I eyed the pacified armadillo in his hold. "So, how do you tame them?"

His mouth twitched. "I'm one of a rare kind." I tilted my head and silently waited for him to expand on that with a brag. People loved to talk about themselves. I just needed to have the patience long enough to let them speak. He cleared his throat and did as I expected. "It's possible to appeal to the familiar's animal side. If you're very good with animals, that is. They have to trust you, and having that natural affinity for wild creatures is very rare. Maybe you could tell your son that's another reason why I'm the familiars professor." I cringed at the memory of Dio's blatant question until a new smell overwhelmed me. Another surge of sandalwood's powerful scent filled the air. Professor Holden certainly enjoyed sharing about this skill of his. "Nobody else could tame the magical animals we brought in. Not without the long and tedious bonding process. Thankfully for your daughter's sake, I think she is part of that slim percentage that I belong to. My hummingbird usually hates kids."

Appeal to the animal side. I could do that. My pet mouse listened to me, plus I was a werewolf—as close to a wolf as one could be. Maybe Mysty would trust me if I shifted into my wolf form and approached her on all fours the way I'd watched

Stevie gain the trust of hundreds of wild animals over the past few years. I could copy the pitchy voice with which she beckoned all manner of creatures. If she was part of that slim percentage, maybe I was too.

A smile tilted my lips, lifting my hope along with it. I flashed a grin at Professor Holden. "This really helps. Thank you." I thrust out my hand in an offer to shake his.

After an awkward moment, he gave it a quick shake and we hurried out of the animal dorms. We had another tricky path to navigate across the campus to the Main Hall, and an even trickier animal familiar to tame, but speaking with Professor Holden left me with a slice of key lime pie's hopeful aroma.

If Ted's spell matched a ghost trap and Madam Rowena was the only one with access to it for the past few weeks, she'd look guiltier than a kid with candy wrappers hidden under their pillow.

CHAPTER 13
WOLF VS. WEREWOLF

EAGER TO FIND COACH, the truth, and the grimoire, I yanked the door to the Main Hall open. That ghost trap spell was the key to confirming Madam Rowena's involvement. She already had the motive to murder. Now the means to kidnap was buried in her filing cabinet and protected by her fierce wolf. Once Hattie spotted Madam Rowena speaking to a group of students in the library, we knew we were in the clear for at least twenty minutes. Twenty minutes to tame a wolf, find the file, and identify it as a ghost trap.

Eyes watched us from the painting of a witch in flare jeans and a tie-dye shirt with the word "peace" splashed across the front. The ghostly chill surrounded us, trailing my every step. Occasionally, I'd glimpse the hem of Jane's skirt or another ghost's elbow or foot.

"Why is Jane following us?" I asked Hattie in a low voice.

Hattie glanced at the movement in the walls and pursed her lips thoughtfully. "She believes you'll find Coach for her. She misses her dreadfully."

The hope I felt earlier heightened, and I felt I was floating alongside my ghostly friend. Jane believed in me. "She doesn't think I'm the murderer?" I whispered.

Hattie shook her head, and the golden headband caught the glow of daylight streaming in through the stained-glass windows. "She trusts me, and I trust you. I did try jogging her memory of you, but it was a long time ago and she's seen a lot of students come and go since then."

"And I wasn't even a student." Of course, I was in a photograph in Shadowvale's walls, so I had *some* connection. Was it too far-fetched to hope it was someone in my family connecting me to this place? Someone involved in the origination of *The Book of Prophecies*?

"Exactly. She said there are others with far greater motive to murder Coach than a scorned applicant. To her, it just sounded silly."

Good. Maybe I could get Officer Harbour to see it that way too. And with enough clues pointing at Madam Rowena, maybe I wouldn't even need to.

We cut into the side hallway, where the plaque on the chief academic officer's door caught my eye. Though the door was shut and locked, Hattie phased through the wall to unhook the latch from the other side. Glancing both ways, I slipped inside and quietly shut the door behind me.

I spun around and faced the wolf's gleaming eyes.

She stood up, fur raised on her back. Before shifting, I tried approaching her slowly. A low growl rumbled from the base of her ribcage. She flashed her sharp teeth as her snout crinkled and twitched.

"It's okay," I said in the same voice my daughter spoke to the crab she'd befriended. "We can be friends. I'm like you." I repeated phrases I'd often heard Stevie say, but the wolf was not appeased. She bared her fangs again, warning me not to get any closer. My heart pounded double time as I extended my hand out in an offering of surrender. Stevie always kept her distance from animals before she reached out her hand and encouraged the creature to come to her.

I turned my palm up. Black lines streaked across my hand like poisoned veins. A gasp escaped me and I yanked my hand back. Mysty didn't like that. She snapped her drooling jaws at the air between us as her back paws danced with edgy energy.

"It's okay," I said again, though I didn't even know if I believed it. With slower movements now, I turned my hand over. Relief washed through me, cold and refreshing. The black marks were only on the surface of my skin. I rubbed at it, but the ink had stained the crude shape of a symbol into my palm. It smudged, but I couldn't wipe it off without some hot water and soap.

Mysty barked, and every nerve inside me jolted. Hattie sucked in a breath and melted into the wall behind me. The wolf couldn't even hurt her, but no doubt she felt the powerful intimidation.

I swallowed and scraped my brain for memories of Stevie. Most of the time she simply talked with the animals. Even when the crab snapped his claws at her, she kept jabbering away as if he was already her new best friend.

I met Mysty's eyes and slowly offered my inky hand again. "We're friends. Wolf to wolf. I know what it's like to be protective of something. I'm very protective of my children. They're not only my pride and joy, they're my only family." Her low growling faded to silence so I kept talking. "They mean everything to me. We're all we have. I mean, we have friends. Hattie and Grandmae and Sett are amazing. They love us like family, and my kids are happy with that."

Mysty's top lip dipped lower and lower until I could no longer see her fangs. I shuffled a few inches closer, hand still out. "They're happy with the friends we've found and turned into family, but..." My voice cracked. Sudden emotion swelled in my throat. Mysty must have sensed it because she dipped her head and then met my gaze again. My heart flipped. Did she understand me? I swallowed through the squeeze in my throat and continued. "But I still want to know who I am. I still want to know if I have a family out there somewhere."

Tears burned at the rims of my eyes. Mysty whimpered. She didn't move from her post, but she stretched her neck enough to sniff at my fingertips. Shaking with emotion more than fear now, I carefully reached my hand to the side of her head. "Maybe they abandoned me because I'm a terrible person." The words flowed now, spilling out of me along with hot tears. The tears rolled down my cheeks and splashed with fat drops to the floor between her paws and my feet. "Maybe I'm as bad as the memory suggests and they had every right to leave me." I didn't even know I'd felt this until the words came out of me.

Mysty sat on her haunches and stared up at me with dewy black puppy eyes. Another whimper invited me to pet her. I buried my hand into the soft fur of her neck and gently scratched. She accepted my touch, so I sank to my knees and wrapped my arms around her the same way I gave my children hugs while they were in their wolf forms.

Wracking sobs consumed me until my head throbbed only a moment later. I needed this. I hadn't realized how broken I'd become when the hope of finding my family disappeared with the grimoire. Disappointment had only been building until it broke the dam of stoicism, and I melted into Mysty in a pile of tears. I gathered myself and pulled away, wiping at my cheeks with the heels of my palms.

"Noema," Hattie whispered, her voice soft for once in her entire ghostly existence. "She's laying down."

Mysty flopped to the side, back paws splayed out to the side to invite more petting down her back and over her belly. A strange laugh bubbled out of me like all of the pent up emotion had just popped. I gave her belly a scratch. Sniffling, I sucked in a full breath and reached for the bottom drawer.

As expected, the spells and essays were filed alphabetically. Ted Moore was at the bottom of the cabinet. I slid the file with his name out and opened the folder. A thick essay was tucked into one side, and on the other side were pages and pages of sketches with mathematics in the margins. Each sketch looked like pieces of a dot-to-dot puzzle. I pulled the pages out and arranged them on the ground between me and Mysty. She watched with mild interest, likely just waiting for more pets.

After shuffling and reshuffling, the pages finally formed a shape—a diamond with drawings of example images. Tiny arrows pointed to the images, and the text written beneath marked them as decoy matter.

"This is it. This is a ghost trap but with the decoy matter for summoning." When Hattie didn't answer, I snapped my head up to see her head was missing. She'd stuck her head through the wall and into the hallway. "Hattie?"

She thrust her head back and whipped around, eyes wide. "Noema, you've got to get out of here. Right now!"

Footsteps approached too quickly. I couldn't move, couldn't think when the doorknob twisted. The door swung open, and Officer Harbour stomped over the threshold, eyes red and watery.

I froze, unable to even breathe.

Madam Rowena followed in his wake, and the group in the hall quickly became a crowd. More ghosts surrounded us inside the walls, making the tight space appear to close in on me. I struggled to draw breath into my lungs. The witch who tried to frame me had arrived, along with the man who could arrest me.

"That fur definitely matches her ears," Madam Rowena said.

For a moment, Officer Harbour only stared at me, and then a frown twisted his face and his wolf ears folded back, defensive and ready to pounce. From werewolf to werewolf, I knew that look. I knew what he'd say before the words came out. My heart fell, matching where I'd landed in life. Rock bottom.

"Noema Wolf," he said, unhooking handcuffs from his belt, "you're under arrest for the murder of Carissa Harbour."

CHAPTER 14
DETAINED AND DREAMING

THOUGH THIS WASN'T the first time I'd seen the inside of a jail cell, I'd never been arrested for murder before. Officer Harbour shoved me into the empty cell and slammed the door after my failed phone call. Though it was my right to have a full phone call—to wait for an answer and actually speak with someone on the other line—Officer Harbour whisked me away from the phone before I got the chance to try Mae or Sett.

I'd used my call for Crow because Hattie didn't have a cell phone, and truthfully, I just needed a hug. I needed Crow to tell me it was going to be okay, but he never answered.

Officer Harbour shook the cell door to double check the lock was securely in place. As if I was some kind of serial murderer...

"I'm not a killer," I said, wishing I could believe it myself. But the memory was still there, and now the cops had evidence.

"Forensics never lies. Your fur was at the crime scene. Inside the damn box."

"Of course it was because I was there. I found the bones." Wait. *Inside?*

"That's my wife you're talking about!" He slammed his fist

against the bars and then cursed. After flexing his hand, he pointed between my eyes. "Where is she?"

I wrapped my fingers around the cold bars and met his gaze. Desperation shook my voice. "That's what I was trying to tell you back in Madam Rowena's office. I don't know where Coach is. Madam Rowena is the one with the access to the ghost trap spell and the summoning spells. The students were working on a whole project. The projects that Madam Rowena oversaw. She also had motive. She wanted to be dean of Shadowvale, but your wife was never going to retire."

He scoffed. "You had access to the spell too. You were holding it, genius."

I winced. He wasn't wrong, but the cruel way he snapped at my intelligence hurt all the same. I was suddenly glad I didn't mention that Madam Rowena also had full control over *The Book of Prophecies* and that meant she probably stole it. Officer Harbour would only flip that back on me.

"You probably won't believe me, but Madam Rowena had a motive to kill and kidnap Coach. She wanted the role as dean. I looked into her because she lied—"

"Ha! Nice try, but your deflection won't work. Madam Rowena already confessed about a fight she and my wife had. She lied because she was scared I'd consider her a suspect." He leaned closer, spittle flying from between his teeth. "You see, normal people lie when they get desperate, they don't kill. I know you got rejected from Shadowvale. Did ya think murdering the dean was going to get you enrolled?" He laughed bitterly. I couldn't deny any of this because I had no proof I didn't do it.

"And if you must know," he said. "The fur at the crime scene? It's thin, from a werewolf's summer coat, not from the winter coat you have now. It didn't get left there when you happened upon her remains."

My mouth fell open, but I had no words. How did my fur end up at the crime scene? I'd never even set foot on this campus before a few days ago. I couldn't even begin to understand. Had Madam Rowena framed me and taken my fur? Or had I turned into a werewolf right after I'd killed Coach all those years ago, and a tuft of my fur was left inside the trunk when I hid her bones? Had I blocked out the memory of burying her remains?

The first thing I remembered was waking in a forest, but I could never recall what forest. The fact that the timeline matched up made me sick. I was young when I turned. That was all I knew.

Officer Harbour shook his head and muttered something I didn't hear. He walked off like that, talking to himself, distraught, before he threw a look over his shoulder and swore he'd be back to interrogate me after he processed my paperwork. "You'll tell me where she is."

With that, he left me alone in the dimly lit cell.

I drew my legs to my chest, curling up at the corner of the dingy cot with my back against the wall. The drafty cell was too cold, even for my hot werewolf tendencies. Or maybe I just hadn't warmed up after the flurry of frustrated ghosts. Jane was distraught over Coach's kidnapping. The ghosts trailed us every step out of Shadowvale whispering *murderer* over and over. Though who they were saying it to was never clear.

My scent and fur were both found near the bones, and that was that.

At least now I knew why Officer Harbour was hell bent against me, though the knowledge didn't do me any good.

Now I waited—or was forced to wait—because I'd been impatient in the past, following smells where I shouldn't, and involving myself in the search for the buried bones. It didn't help that I had no alibi for the night they suspected the hand bone was stolen. The kids had been at a sleepover, leaving me home alone and with no witnesses. The odds were stacked against me, and now I was locked up and my only company was the tick of the clock on the wall outside my cell. The rhythmic sound triggered an ache in my heart for the Swiss Army Watch Crow had given me. It was stored away somewhere in this station with the rest of my belongings.

Though it was late into the night, I couldn't sleep. Every time I closed my eyes, I saw the wolf print and the picture of myself all those years ago—before I was a wolf. Was I turned just so that a killer could frame me? Had Madam Rowena forced me to drink rainwater out of another werewolf's paw print to turn me?

Finally, I drifted into a fitful sleep where nightmares plagued me. Nightmares about the first time I'd woken up as a werewolf. Only days later, I ran into Christopher. He liked to say it was love at first bite, but the inside joke didn't make sense since we fell in love long before he accidentally became a were-wolf, and of course, I didn't bite. Instead, it was a mere scratch that I'd left on his hand when I was too clumsy on two feet. I slipped on a puddle, and when he went to grab me, my instincts were to shift to all four paws to break my fall. My claws extended, gashing his arm and hand, and the rest was history. A happy story of two werewolves who fell in love all over again. Until a medical emergency ended in tragedy. Traces of silver in the antibiotics the doctors gave Christopher only made him sicker, and I was left a single mom with four young children.

I could still hear him insist that it was meant to be, even after I told him about how he'd become a werewolf and that it was my fault. *"I found you again because we're soulmates. Noema, I'm here for you always."*

The voice came alive, deep and slicing through the dream of a life lived years ago.

"Noema, I'm here—"

I shot up on the creaky cot. I almost expected to see my late husband through the sleep in my eyes. But the sight of the cold bars on the jail cell jolted me back to reality, and the face on the other side wasn't Christopher's. I blinked sleep away as my eyes focused on the broad-shouldered gargoyle in a navy coat and black jeans. Concern creased the space between Sett's slate eyes until he broke his gaze and moved out of the way for another officer.

The chief of police unlocked the cell and the door swung open with a squeak. "You're free to go," he said, voice filled with irritation. The surrounding air matched his anger with the heady odor of smoke.

Tentatively, I scooted to the edge of the cot and stood. "What's going on?" I looked between both police officers. "How did you know I was here?"

Sett cleared his throat and stepped halfway into the cell, extending his hand. "Hattie hitched a ride on a bus to come and get me. She's helping Bette take care of business at Mockbuster now. Here, let's get you out of there, and I'll explain the rest."

Officer Harbour left us as I took Sett's hand and we maneuvered through the police station, stopping only to process my release and gather my belongings. I didn't let myself believe the good news until we were outside in the crisp winter breeze. I relished the fresh air, though it did nothing to warm me after a night spent in the chilly cell. Cold or not, at least I'd gotten a full night's sleep. The sun tried to peer through the patchy clouds as if to greet me upon my release to freedom.

I finally took a breath and turned to Sett. "Okay, explain. Last I heard you were annoyed with me for involving myself. I was suspect number one for Coach's murder, and, let's face it, you were right. I never should've gotten so involved, and I'm honestly speechless that you're here to bail me out."

Sett cracked a smile, and I almost wanted to sock him right in the shoulder for being amused over my confusion. Or maybe he was enjoying the pride of being right. Either way, I couldn't help but fold my arms in a lame attempt to defend myself from his *I told you so* attitude. He tapped a finger to his lips before speaking. "Noema, you can't be both speechless and talking at the same time."

I threw up my arms. "You got me there! You're right again. And what's with that stupid gesture?" I mimicked him by tapping my finger to my lips.

"I don't know, I just meant you're always talking. You're not quiet."

"So?"

"So, that's fine, talking is what gets answers and truth. I like answers and truth."

"Good thing I'm not"—I mimicked the gesture again—"quiet then right?"

"Are you mad that I'm here?"

I wasn't. Not really. Not at all. I was emotionally exhausted after the interrogation and the nightmares and perturbed by the bad timing of his amusement. My anger was misguided and my behavior childish. I frowned apologetically. "I just don't know how to say thank you or how I'll pay you back."

"Noema." There it was again, like the voice I heard in my dreams. I paused, letting him continue to walk into the parking lot without me. He headed for his car, and I jogged to meet up with him when he spoke again. "I'm here to help you. And the good news is, there was no bail because you didn't commit a crime."

"I didn't?"

He cocked his head, eyeing me over the top of the car as we stood at opposite doors. And then he nodded, understanding dawning in his eyes. "You don't remember. That's why I'm here."

"Because you're my back up?" I referred to the near-nickname we'd once called each other in a time and place that felt like a far away galaxy. Maybe I'd watched too many science fiction movies with Sett.

"Because you're a turned werewolf and someone can easily frame you," he said as we climbed into the car. Our elbows bumped into each other across the center console. If he noticed, he didn't seem to care. He shifted the car into reverse, throwing his hand behind me on the head rest as he backed out of the parking space. Easing out of the parking lot, he continued. "The timing was wrong. You'd remember being at Shadowvale if you'd already become a werewolf. So I researched your name with the last initial "T" after Hattie gave me a call about your arrest. I found a Noema Titan"

He paused, knowing I'd need to let that sink in. Titan was the same name mentioned in *The Book of Prophecies* regarding a family of witches. Absently, I lifted my hand and traced the tattoo mark on my collarbone. Speculations were now confirmed, but I didn't have the emotional wherewithal to process it. All I could think about was that I had a last name to search records with now. Had Sett found my family?

As if reading my mind, he glanced at me, mouth twisted. Earthy sadness wafted from him with the scent of fresh rain. "Most records of Noema Titan seem to be erased, and I couldn't find anyone else with the same last name. I'm sorry, Noema."

I shrugged, this time truly speechless. It was a long shot anyway. My last name was erased from Shadowvale's documents, so why did I expect other records to be any different? He cleared his throat and softened his voice.

"But I did find you in a newspaper article. The photograph was clearly you before you became a werewolf."

"An article about what?"

Sett kept his eyes on the road as he reached behind me and produced a folder. I left it on my lap, staring at it for a moment. Opening the cover, I found printed pieces of paper neatly placed in the pockets. At first, I couldn't get past the article's title.

"Young Woman Defies Death When a Bullet Bounces Off Scarf." My eyes flew across the article, though the title was almost everything I needed to know. At the bottom, a picture of the younger, non-werewolf me stared back, smiling. I wore a crocheted scarf the same shade as the fur I got once I became a werewolf. The pepper gray was plain, almost ugly, but apparently the yarn was what had saved my life against a hunter's gun.

"This article is dated after Carissa Harbour's death," Sett said, driving with one hand as he pointed at the paper. "No wolf ears means no wolf fur. It would be impossible for you to leave that evidence. Noema, you were framed."

Ice filled my veins as I sat rigid in the passenger seat, staring helplessly at the newspaper print. Had Madam Rowena framed me long before I ever realized? Finally able to form words again, I spilled everything I knew, everything that'd happened at Shadowvale, everything I could possibly think to tell Sett, and when I finished, gravel crunched beneath the car and a long shadow cast by the Main Hall stretched over us.

Sett had driven us back to Shadowvale.

"What are we doing here?" I expected to be taken home and encouraged to leave the investigation to the Caldale police.

Sett turned the keys until the car's engine died, and then he yanked them from the ignition. "Officer Harbour has agreed that he's too emotional and too close to this case. Since I've offered my help to the Caldale police department, we need to figure this out." He reached across the center console and gave my hand an unexpected squeeze. "If Madam Rowena is the one who did this, we'll find out. Let's have a chat with her, and you can smell for the truth."

Emotion knotted in my throat. We'd saved each other's lives before, and in little ways, we'd backed each other up. I always stocked his favorite candy on Mockbuster's snack wall. He always waited to watch new releases until I had time to watch them with him. We'd been one another's backup, sure, but never like this. Sett came all this way, involving himself in an investigation and now asking for my support. Of course he was still playing by the rules and only working on the case after having received Caldale Police Department's blessing. Despite the surprise, he was still Sett.

And I was still Noema. Not a killer, but perhaps a little too curious.

SHADOWVALE WAS QUIET, empty. Nobody perused the front of the school, no voices echoed from the gardens or the courtyard. We exchanged a look over the car and then headed up the steps of the Main Hall. Inside, ghosts flurried in and out of the walls, echoing with screams and restless chatter.

We marched up and down the changing halls, checking the lobby, and near the offices. Nobody was to be found. Nobody alive, anyway.

I squinted at a painting of Coach, recognizing the hum of Jane's voice, though she spoke too quietly for me to understand her.

"Jane?" I said. "Where is everyone?"

She stepped out of the painting, materializing into her full shape. "They're preparing to leave," she said. "We've condemned Shadowvale."

"What?"

"I believe Madam Rowena killed Coach, but the officers are useless." Her brow furrowed to a sharp angle, and her eyes narrowed. "They won't listen to us, so I've taken matters into my own hands."

Sett stepped in front of me as a protective shield against the ghost who was now wearing a terrifying and threatening grin. "What does that entail?" he asked.

She smoothed her long skirt and then leveled Sett's gaze. "Madam Rowena says we're dangerous, so she's ordered for all of the students to leave the school until we've calmed down. Now that she's in charge, she's throwing her weight around. It is really rather offensive to the likes of us who have no weight."

"She's in charge?" I asked.

Did Madam Rowena finally make her dream come true?

Jane nodded, a frown now twisting her lips. "Coach is gone, so Madam Rowena swooped in to steal her role. I am livid. Just livid!" She blew through us, frost crystalizing in her wake. Her ghostly presence left both of us shivering and breathless. If she'd lingered, we could have frozen, and both of us were people who *liked* the cold. I couldn't imagine how quickly the ghost could have given frostbite to someone who wasn't an overheated werewolf or naturally chilly gargoyle. Maybe Madam Rowena was right to condemn the university until the ghosts were under control.

Sett puffed with a coil of icy air as he turned on his heels. "You said they're preparing to leave; where is everyone now?"

"Dorm rooms!" Jane shouted, her voice a shrill screech to my sensitive ears. She vanished inside Madam Rowena's office, and I could only imagine what she wanted to do to it if she solidified long enough to tear it apart.

To add to the list of surprises today, Sett actually kept pace with me. The slow-moving gargoyle was my opposite, always thinking too long before he acted. Today, he matched me step-for-step, and I barged into the girls' building while he went to the guys' dorms to search for Madam Rowena. Professors oversaw the students as they packed go bags and hurried down the stairs. I waded through the bustle of college kids, scanning for Madam Rowena's unmistakable posture. But she wasn't here, just students with heavy bags.

I spotted Alicia's blonde ponytail as she shoved out the door, a duffle bag slung over one shoulder. I dove after her, ducking past elbows and overstuffed luggage.

"Alicia!"

She spun around. Spotting me, her eyes widened and she stepped back. "Aren't you like a murderer or something?"

I huffed, catching my breath as I stopped in front of her. "No. Not at all, I have an alibi." It felt good to say aloud. "Have you seen Madam Rowena?"

She shook her head, ponytail swishing. "Not since she called us to the auditorium. She announced that the school is shutting down until the investigation is over or the ghosts agree to back off."

"Do you think she left campus?"

Alicia shrugged, then hiked the duffle bag's strap higher on her shoulder. "She should; the ghosts have it out for her. Professor Holden was right about them.They're insanely annoying." Ted came up to her, standing beside her with a furrowed brow as he raked his gaze over me.

"Not a murderer," I said.

"Cool." He tilted his chin.

"Do you know where Madam Rowena would be?" I asked.

"Ask one of the professors. They know more than we do," he said

"Okay, thank you. Are you all going home?"

"Nope." Alicia beamed. "We get to stay in hotels paid for by the school. It's so rad. Except for the fact that now we have to wait longer to present our senior spells."

"How come?"

She scoffed. "Obviously we're not allowed to perform new magic off campus."

"Is it dangerous to do that?"

She shrugged again. "No, it's just the rules, and Madam Rowena would die if we didn't follow every stupid boring rule. It's like her personality or something, which is like *yawn*, you know?" A personality like that sounded all too familiar. Sett followed rules like it was his personality too, and as much as it got in my way, I appreciated his moral code now. I could always trust him. "Anyway, this conversation is painfully boring, so bye!" Her voice pitched higher at the end and she forced a smile before abandoning me.

Ted rolled his eyes and leaned closer to me as if we shared a secret. "Alicia just wants to brag that her project is finished, but she doesn't even know if Madam Rowena will accept the spell's concept yet."

"What do you mean? Doesn't Madam Rowena have all the spells that are already turned in?"

"They're stored in her office, but it's tradition that no judge touches them until presentation day. She even calls off her guard dog for exactly five minutes so that each student can file the folders on their own. That way she doesn't risk accidentally seeing anything that could sway her judgment on presentation day."

I nodded, mulling this over when Ted shouted to a friend

across the courtyard. I folded my ears back from the painfully loud sound of his voice and turned away from him.

Sett arrived beside me just after Ted vanished into the sea of students. "She's not in the guys' dorms."

I spotted a human professor the tour guide had introduced us to on that first day. I squeezed past two warlocks and called out to him. "Professor Thompson!"

He frowned. When I caught up with him, he looked me up and down. "Parents are not allowed on campus at this time, you can meet up with your son or daughter at the hotel—"

"Excuse me? I am *not* old enough to have a child in college."

Sett sidled up beside me, having taken longer to pick his way through the tight crowd. "She's really not. And she definitely doesn't act like it."

I shoved an elbow into his ribcage, but I was the one who gasped. Damn his stupid stony body. Professor Thompson only blinked at us, utterly uninterested.

"I'm looking for Madam Rowena."

He laughed. "She locked herself inside Coach's office and warded it against the ghosts. Good luck getting to her before the ghosts freeze you to death."

"Do you know why she's staying on campus?"

"She's acting dean now; she won't abandon it. I assume she's working on a way to ward the entire campus against the ghosts."

But why go through all this trouble when nobody seemed to be afraid of the ghosts? None of the bits of conversation I caught were about the ghosts either. So why condemn the entire campus when the ghosts mostly stayed in the Main hall? I supposed Ted and Alicia were mildly annoyed but not nearly enough if it delayed graduation and, as a result, the start of their lives.

Were Alicia and Ted right? Was Madam Rowena always so adamant about following rules? The question buzzed in my mind as Professor Thompson lost interest in us and wandered away, directing two shapeshifters and a half dragon to the parking lot.

"What are you thinking?" Sett asked. "We're not going through that hall again. Another ghost swipe and we could get seriously sick from the cold."

I shook my head. "No, we can't go in there again."

"We can call her and have her come meet us," he suggested. "From the safety of the motel."

"The motel?" I looked up at him.

"Come on, we both need to rest."

CHAPTER 15
ONE BED, PLENTY OF PIZZA

THE EMPLOYEE behind the desk at Lunar Motel flicked his shoulder-length hair from his face and smirked before he turned to grab the key off of an old-fashioned pegboard. He smelled odd and acted about the same, eyes unfocused and a bit out of it like the characters in *Dazed and Confused*. Or maybe Shaggy from "Scooby Doo." He halfway tripped over the desk chair when he turned back, key pinched in his hand. Chuckling, he winked at Sett and said, "You got the last room left when you called. King-sized bed."

Sett's lips flattened and he furrowed his brow. A hint of pineapple pizza-scented confusion trickled from him. When the Shaggy dude glanced between us, my pulse pitched. He thought we were getting the room for a night *together*.

I dared to peer at Sett again to see if he understood. The smell of confusion was gone, but he ignored the employee and started for the stairs. I followed in his wake, wondering where we'd both sleep.

On the stairs, he craned his neck, looking down at me. "I didn't expect every hotel to be booked up around here." His voice was tight, and I caught a whiff of an odd mixture: truth's lavender, a dash of pungent nerves, and a smell almost like the vanilla-scent of books. I never used to be able to smell Sett's emotions, but I could smell this. Was it getting easier, or did I just know him better?

We climbed to the second floor and stopped in front of room 205. He fiddled with the key, sliding it into the lock before he twisted, and the door creaked open. The large bed filled most of the space, and a box TV was perched opposite the headboard on a small stand. Two nightstands flanked the bed, and the closest wall opened into a bathroom. If we weren't on the bed, there was nowhere else to be, other than maybe the bathtub.

He cleared his throat. "I'm sorry I couldn't find a better hotel."

I laid my hand on his arm. "Sett, you came all the way out here to help me. Don't apologize for anything. And there's nothing you can do about the availability; I think the hotels are booked up with Shadowvale students."

He nodded with a heavy swallow, then turned and stepped into the room. I followed, carrying with me the hint of my own nerves as my chest fluttered. Thoughts of our almost-kiss months ago needled me along with memories of when I'd fallen asleep on his shoulder, and that time he scooped me up and out of the way of a fire. Did he ever think of those moments between us? I'd been alone with Sett in the car, at the Bewitcher's Beach police station, and sometimes at my shop, but never in a bedroom.

What would Crow think? Surely he'd be jealous, but I couldn't exactly sleep outside in the cold. He'd understand there were no other rooms available, and that sharing with Sett was a necessity. Wouldn't he? Did it matter? He could be the one here helping me if he'd answered my call.

Once inside, we both stood at opposite sides of the bed.

Neither of us was willing to climb into the bed first, though it was clear we were both exhausted. My arms hung at my sides like two sacks of sand, and Sett's eyes looked heavy. The ghost's nervous energy was enough to suck the life out of anyone. No doubt he was beat after staying up late to find my proof of innocence and then driving all the way out here. He was a good detective, thorough and thoughtful to dig into this investigation and find the thread that provided my alibi. A really good detective.

I dragged the slight point of my canine against my bottom lip, resisting the urge to flop onto the bed. I couldn't be selfish and take it, not after all he did for me—or for my case. But I felt myself sinking into the mattress, leaning into it with my legs and waist. What would it be like to sleep side-by-side with Sett? His natural chill keeping my overheated body cool.

He was here for me. All the way in Caldale, hours away from home. Even if it was his nature as a detective to find the truth, he didn't have to accept my help. He could have dumped me back home and returned to help Caldale police department, but he didn't. He was here standing in front of me, and I couldn't help but hear Christopher's voice and smell a hint of vanilla. *Noema, I'm here for you.*

Sett rubbed the back of his neck and then swooped his hand out as an offer for me to hop in the bed. "You should get some rest while I call Madam Rowena. I'm willing to bet that cot was uncomfortable." I opened my mouth, but my stomach responded before I could say anything, growling loud enough to be its own werewolf. Groans of hunger sliced through the tension, and I couldn't help the laugh that bubbled out of me. Sett chuckled and reached for the phone on the nightstand at his side of the bed. "I guess I'll order us a pizza first."

I tapped my finger to my lips. "Not even my stomach knows how to be quiet."

When he laughed again and returned the gesture as he picked up the phone, I finally allowed myself to pull up one leg and sit on the edge of the bed. The soft mattress sank beneath my weight and my limbs pulled heavier, beckoning for me to drop my head on the pillow and descend into the fluffy comfort. But the thought of food reinvigorated me, and as soon as Sett finished ordering, we could call Madam Rowena.

How would Madam Rowena know that I'd come back to Shadowvale all these years later? If she framed me when she killed Coach, like the lies she spewed to Officer Harbour, had she somehow tricked me into coming back here? Was the field trip her idea? It was too far-fetched even for me. I loved a good twisty mystery on stage—heck, I wanted to write it for the big screen someday—but even this wouldn't make a good story. *Coincidences never do.*

I didn't know what to ask her when she met up with us, but I trusted that ideas would come once I had food in my belly.

Sett covered the mouthpiece and whispered. "Extra pepperoni?"

I smiled at the fact that he remembered my preference. There wasn't a pizza place in Bewitcher's Beach, but I'd bought ingredients from the grocery next to Mockbuster and customized a pizza one night when he watched *Space Jam* with me and the kids. Nodding, I said, "And ranch sauce."

"Make it extra large." He glanced at me, half smile on his usually-stoic face. Apparently food boosted his mood too. Of course it did; Sett was as good a chef as he was a detective. Slow at both, though.

By the time the pizza arrived, we'd both splashed water on our faces and sat on the bed, discussing the details of Coach's death, Madam Rowena's behavior, and motives. He'd allowed himself to relax with both legs on the bed, one curled under him, and his back against the headboard, his hand behind his head to cushion it against the wooden headboard. I sat with my legs crossed, elbows on knees.

Sett leaned forward and took another piece of pizza, the cheese stringing long as it stayed attached to the pie. Hot and gooey, it dripped back into the cardboard box as he plucked it from the tip of the slice and then took a bite. Swallowing, he said, "Let me make sure I understand all this before I call her. So Madam Rowena may have killed Coach in an attempt to become the next dean?"

I nodded and took a sip of my Diet Pepsi. The ice sloshed around in the paper cup as I leaned over to set it on the nightstand. "Both Senna and Jane said Madam Rowena wanted to be dean."

"But killing Coach didn't help."

I set my slice of pizza back in the box and wiped the grease off my fingers with a napkin. "Right. They didn't talk about Coach's death or anything during the field trip obviously." I waved my hand.

"Obviously," he repeated.

"But from what I gleaned during the field trip, Coach was an extremely powerful witch when she was alive. So much so that as a ghost, she retained intricate magic that even live witches and warlocks haven't been able to touch since." He cocked his head, eating and listening. "Magical animals can share traces of their power to anyone they trust, but Coach could borrow complete power from a familiar, even familiars that weren't hers. So she attracted the most powerful familiars. All magical animals within her vicinity would boost her ability to cast spells, which I guess isn't something anyone else can do as well as her. And according to Shadowvale's history, witches with familiars always become ghosts until their familiar dies or bonds with someone else. Then they can pass on."

"And Madam Rowena would have known that."

"Right." Madam Rowena was too sharp to do something as stupid as go up against the most powerful witch. Even if she *did* want to become dean and even if that dean was technically dead. "She would have had to kill or bond with every familiar Coach ever cast magic with in order to ensure Coach didn't become a ghost."

Sett sighed and tilted his head, cracking his neck on both sides. "That's a lot of work on top of framing you, and just to become dean."

"And she isn't even around Coach's familiars."

My stomach was finally happy, but I wasn't. It was cozy, comfortable even, to be curled up on the bed beside the man who was here for me. But comfort didn't solve why my fur had ended up by a dead body. Something wasn't adding up, and it felt we were getting further from the truth as the thin theory regarding Madam Rowena frayed.

I uncrossed my legs and leaned against the headboard, finally full. To fit side-by-side, our shoulders touched. I turned to meet his gaze. "She lied to Officer Harbour about me, and Jane believes Coach's spirit still exists somewhere, maybe caught in a ghost trap created by a student's senior spell." Memories of being trapped in a summoning diamond sent a shiver down my spine. "There has to be a reason for Madam Rowena's lie, and the senior spells had to be mashed together by someone with access to them. She's the one who grades all the senior spells."

"So Madam Rowena instructs students to create the spells she needs and then steals the work—"

I yanked my legs in and sat up pin-straight, the action causing Sett to stop talking mid-sentence. "Wait. I was so distracted and well—" I waved at the pizza. "Starving too obviously, my brain wasn't working. Alicia said they can't even perform their senior spells yet."

"Would they have worked with Madam Rowena on them before their presentation?"

I shook my head. "I don't think so. Ted said they don't know if she'll even accept the concept."

"You're thinking she didn't look at the ghost trap spell?"

"I'm thinking I'm confused. I need to ask if she actually follows the tradition that she won't touch the spells until presentation day. According to the students, she doesn't even know what their spells are about. Then I can smell for the truth." This could actually work to get answers. Key lime pie sweetened the air around me.

Excited for answers, I practically climbed into Sett's lap to reach the phone. Heat burned my cheeks as I hopped off the bed and plucked hair from my face. I flashed an apologetic smile for climbing over him and then reached for the phone, dialing the number for Coach's office. A number I memorized after calling to ask about the progress on the grimoire. "I can't wait any longer; I'm calling her." The other line trilled and trilled and trilled. With each unanswered ring, my shoulders sagged, and a whiff of rain filled the air around me as disappointment set in.

"Hello?" Madam Rowena's voice finally cut through the white noise of the constant ringing.

I straightened, gripping the phone tighter. "Madam Rowena, it's Noema."

A rush of air blew into the receiver. "I heard you were released. What do you want from me?"

"I'm hoping you might meet me at Lunar Motel to talk with me about something."

"No offense, but I haven't got time for you" Her tone was frazzled, at the edge of her nerves.

Now what was I going to do? I couldn't smell her emotions over the phone.

"What if I meet you outside Shadowvale? All you have to do is leave the Main Hall."

An uncomfortable laugh burst from the other line. "Is that all? Noema, I'm blocked in by a hundred angry ghosts who blame me for murder because of something you told them." Bitterness laced her every word.

"I didn't—Uh." I widened my eyes at Sett, but he couldn't hear her vitriol. What could I say now? She refused to meet with us, and we couldn't go into that hallway. If I sicked Sett on her as a police investigator, would she do something dangerous out of desperation? I'd jumped into this too quickly. Of course.

A forceful sigh came from the other line. Madam Rowena was losing patience, and it was now or never. I couldn't smell her emotions, but I had to ask. She'd probably hang up if I tried to call again.

"Since I was hoping to help Senna practice her spell, I was wondering how much time she had before they perform the oral portion, and if her spell's concept was accepted. I can't remember, have you graded their research essays yet?" Geez, the lies were coming out too easily now. My canine dug into the soft flesh of my lip as I waited for her response.

Another sigh. "No. The rulebook states that the grading witch must not engage with any portion of the senior projects until assessment day so that there is no preconceived judgment. I don't know what they are until they're presented to me, so you can tell Senna to just keep practicing." She said it robotically, as if she'd repeated this a dozen times to a dozen different students who may have asked for her help.

I wished I could sniff for a lie. Madam Rowena had proven herself dishonest before, but Ted was the one who'd said it first. He had no motive to lie about the process for the senior spells, and as a senior, he'd know the traditions. Plus, Alicia swore Madam Rowena was a boring hag for all the traditions and rules she stuck with. Maybe she truly never looked at Ted's spell.

Then who had?

"Okay, thanks." Before she sighed again, or snapped at me, I jammed the phone back on the receiver. I shared everything with my co-detective—not that I was actually a detective—but Sett took in each detail.

"It makes her a lot less suspicious, but it doesn't prove Madam Rowena didn't kill her," he said. I must have visibly drooped because I knew he couldn't smell my disappointment. Sett cleared his throat and continued. "But, we're forgetting one very important question. Why now?"

I cocked my head at him as he threw his legs over the side of the bed. Now we were both in the cramped space on the far side of the bed, facing one another. Close enough that if I lifted my arms and bent at the elbows, I'd be hugging him. I swallowed the nerves buzzing in my throat.

"What's different now that made Madam Rowena kidnap Coach's spirit after all these years?" he asked. "It wasn't the ability to kidnap a ghost because we're assuming she didn't have access to the spells like tradition says, and we know Coach was too powerful for Madam Rowena to simply waltz in and take her tether."

"And she could have tried bonding with Coach's familiars to finally make Coach pass on."

"Exactly. So what's different right now?"

In a moment of silence, I could almost hear the wheels turning. Sett's wings twitched the way they always did when he was about to expand them. He never spread them out unless he was using them as protection. In the past, his wings had blocked me from the elements, from being naked in the woods, and from angry ghosts, but there was no need to shield me from anything in this cozy hotel room.

Sett's brow furrowed, the movement catching my attention. The worried look matched the nervous twitch of his wings, like he wanted to protect me. All at once, the answer came to me.

"I know what's different now." When I spoke, he did too, having come to the same conclusion. "The protection spell."

If the spell was recreated and cast over Shadowvale as a test before returning it to its original place in Bewitcher's Beach—which was what the witches planned to do—all intent to harm someone else on campus would be thwarted. And stealing familiars right out from under Coach was definitely intent to harm.

I shook my head. "That doesn't feel right. The protection spell was Madam Rowena's pride and joy. *She* delivered *The Book of Prophecies* straight to Shadowvale and jump-started the study of it."

Sett hummed his agreement. "That's true. The ingredients aren't mixing. Why do all that just to steal the grimoire and disrupt the study of the protection spell?"

I sank to the edge of the bed, eyes fixed on the drab curtains. "If she killed Coach all those years ago to become dean and then spent all this time trying to kidnap her spirit, she sure as heck wouldn't bring a spell here that'd stop her from doing that."

Sett folded his arms as he stared into the void. Thoughts practically shifted across his slate eyes as he considered this. "People do stupid things sometimes. Do you believe she just didn't think it through? Maybe she was too excited with the discovery of the grimoire?"

Madam Rowena do something stupid? Not a chance in hell. Sett didn't know her as well as I did. He didn't know that suggesting *The Madam Rowena* made a mistake was an absolutely wild and unbelievable theory. At least not a mistake this obvious.

"She didn't kill Coach," I said, relenting. I didn't have evidence, but now that I finally slowed down—now that I finally had an alibi and wasn't pursued by the chief of police— my brain worked well enough to understand that this theory never made sense. If I'd had my head screwed on straight, I'd have put these threads together a long time ago. I wouldn't have wasted time trying to find out if Madam Rowena was the killer.

"You believe this?"

"I do. She's way too smart and too calculated to thwart her own plan. Honestly, she's a lot like you." I looked up at him. Curiosity swam in his eyes. "She follows rules meticulously, and I know that even if you messed up and did something horrible, you'd still follow the rules. Just like she's doing now with the senior spell tradition."

"Okay." Sett nodded. "I trust you know what you're talking about." Warmth bloomed across my chest and crawled up to linger at the curve of my cheeks. Sett was listening to me now more than ever. "You wouldn't give up on someone if they were truly a suspect. This means I need to tell Officer Harbour's team not to waste resources investigating her. I've no doubt they're running ragged, going over everyone who has ever been at Shadowvale. This will at least tie up one loose end for them."

"Right," I said. "And I should tell Jane so she and the other ghosts can calm down and let the students return. Plus, I've been dying to try to find the grimoire's scent again. Now that Officer Harbour isn't on my tail, I think I can track its trail through the woods. The scent I caught was too strong to come from that little scrap of paper alone. *The Book of Prophecies* had to be close by." Once I found the grimoire, we'd have Coach, and she'd be able to tell us who did all this. No investigation or ragged detectives needed. Officer Harbour had said his team already scraped the entire woods for his wife, but they didn't have a connection to *The Book of*

Prophecies—one of the items surely used to summon her—like I did.

"I know you can too. Let's do this." Though his voice was warm and confident, his jaw flexed, and his brow twitched. I couldn't read what he was thinking, but he smelled of fear. The scent of confidence quickly replaced it.

"What?" I asked, breaking the silence that hung between us.

He shook his head. "I wanted to say it's too dangerous and that we shouldn't go back there, but you can handle yourself if the ghosts get dangerous."

I can? I'd just been arrested for murder only a day ago. For once, I wouldn't have blamed Sett if he wanted to stop me. I'd made a lot of mistakes here, but maybe I could help get the students back to their dorms and return everything to normal. Filled with gratitude, I grabbed his hand and laced my fingers through his, giving it a quick squeeze. But when I went to pull my hand back, he held on tighter.

"Noema..." He tugged me closer, the space between us shrinking and shrinking. My heart flipped as I tilted my chin back, drawn to the raw tone in his voice. His gaze dropped to my lips, where it lingered for a moment. I grazed my top teeth over my bottom lip, finding my own eyes falling to his mouth. When he lifted his hand, my breath caught, waiting for him to tip my chin back. Instead, his hand hovered between us, not quite touching my face. "You know I'll always back you up, right?"

I sucked in a breath and gave him a faint nod.

"Good. I'll be right there with you while you face Jane and the other ghosts."

"You're always there for me." The truth slipped out. He'd shown up for me. He'd researched for me. He'd come all the way out here, and now he proved he believed in me.

Finally, and with the slightest touch, the side of his index finger brushed my chin. His touch beckoned me closer as his face dipped a breath away from mine. Thick air, heavy with waiting and wanting, hovered between us.

A blaring ring jarred us from the haze, and I quickly stepped back. Sett drew a sharp breath and then dug his cell phone out of his coat pocket. Scrubbing the back of his neck with one hand, he pressed the device to his ear with the other. His eyes raked over me as he answered the call. "Officer Lawrence here."

I bit my lip before tugging my gaze from him. We'd almost kissed. *We'd almost kissed* and I was still dating Crow.

"An arrest? Doctor Leek?" he said, drawing my attention back. His brow knitted together. "What motive does she have?"

Arrest? It must have been the station calling to inform their out-of-town consultant. But this couldn't mean they arrested Doctor Leek, right?

I laid my hand on Sett's arm. "She's innocent," I said, not caring that I may have interrupted the officer on the other line. They needed to know what I'd smelled. Doctor Leek told nothing but the truth when Hattie had confronted her.

Sett covered the receiver and looked at me. As soon as I relayed the information about Doctor Leek's innocence, he nodded. "You asked her directly?

"Hattie did," I said. He huffed a half smile, knowing how transparent our ghostly friend was with her thoughts. "I smelled the truth."

"Then I have to go set this straight right now, but I..." His voice died away as his eyes searched mine. Based on the faint apology in his eyes, I anticipated what he wanted to say.

"Take me to the school. I'll be okay until you get back."

So maybe I hadn't totally rid myself of impatience.

Answers were too close. All I had to do was get the ghosts to calm down while the investigators found Coach's real killer.

CHAPTER 16
THE TRAIL TO TRUTH

DUST PUFFED from the tires of Sett's car as he drove through the black iron gates of Shadowvale's entrance. I watched until he was out of sight, gathering my courage to go face the angry ghosts and aware that I was the only one here other than the woman who'd framed me. Not even the security guards were perched at the Grand Library anymore. Just me, the ghosts, and the head witch. Pungent ammonia rose from my glands but was quickly swept away when I caught the faint scent of cinnamon sweetness in the air.

"The grimoire," I whispered as if I were a witch and could conjure it from nothing. But nope. I could only claim the power of smell. A very powerful sense of smell.

I took another long whiff and noted the hints of rose perfume. This was definitely the trail for *The Book of Prophecies*. Without the hundreds of students milling about with their angsty emotions stinking up the place, I had a full smell of the trail. Only my own anxious excitement mingled with the scent.

Tentatively, I took a step toward the trees. I didn't want to risk losing the trail. Every few steps, I paused to test if the scent grew stronger or waned. Based on that, I adjusted my direction and drew closer to the forest's edge.

Shadows played with my mind, snapping my attention left and right when I needed to plunge straight ahead and deeper into the darkness. I closed my eyes to block the distractions and carefully followed the trail.

The aroma of rose perfume built and built, and the cinnamon scent tickled my nose until a sneeze overcame me. I drew in another deep breath and pressed forward. It was tedious to step through the forest with my eyes closed, but I refused to lose the trail.

You can be patient.

Or I could drop to all fours and use my keener sense of smell. As a wolf, though, distractions were even more tempting. Animal instinct might have me itching to run. Movement in the shadows or a snapped twig could derail me. Every sense was heightened when I shifted to my werewolf self. No, slow and steady would have to do.

A dull pinch of sandalwood's aroma came from my dredged confidence. Around it, I sniffed for the trail and forged on, eyes still sealed shut so I could focus on smell and only smell. The scent grew, strengthening to a thick and blanketing aroma. I was close. *The Book of Prophecies* was likely lying open only a few feet away now.

I opened my eyes to find I was no longer in the forest. The trees were gone, but the shadows remained. Night was at its darkest now. My eyesight sharpened to the darkness, and I made out the shape of my surroundings.

No trees, no bushes, nothing but wide open space covered in nightfall. A sharp rise of ground lifted into a rocky hill in front of me. An inlet shrouded in black beckoned my curiosity. With only a few more loping steps, I hiked into the damp cave and froze.

Inside the crowded space, a book lay splayed open on the ground, soaked from the enduring moisture and occasional rainfall. Ruined pages curled in on themselves. Pages I recognized. Pages that held the secrets of my past.

My heart lurched, and I ripped my gaze from the destroyed grimoire to the spirit beyond. Coach's ghostly form lay crumpled in hopelessness. Items sat at each of the other three points of the diamond shape drawn into the ground around her. The bones from her hand, a glittering wedding ring, and an animal's leash. Each item had served to summon and trap her. The diamond trap, the hand bones, it was all insurance to keep the spirit of the most powerful witch of our time from breaking free.

With my chest tight and thick anticipation coating my throat, I didn't breathe until I crouched and gently pushed the grimoire aside to break the shape of the diamond.

Mist coiled in front of me as I finally took a gasping breath that roused Coach. Her ghostly shape rose from the heap of sadness on the floor. She floated at the center of the diamond, mirroring me with wide hopeful eyes. Her beautiful round face, glowing rosy cheeks, and bob-cut auburn hair perfectly matched the painting I'd seen of Coach during the field trip tour. My heart fluttered, the smell of hope and excitement and relief rising around me. She was truly a sight to behold with a naturally commanding presence and a radiating magic around her like static electricity. The hair on my arms stood on end and goosebumps pricked. She was the spitting image of what Molly Ringwald might look like as a middle-aged woman. The same actress I hoped would star in my screenplay someday. If I ever wrote it. In her transparent hands, she cupped the footbag tether. Whoever had trapped her here must not have been powerful enough to pry it from her cold, ghostly hands. She'd kept it safe, and her spirit alive. Well, existing, not exactly alive.

Coach's doe eyes widened, and it suddenly hit me. Did she recognize me? I opened my mouth, though I had nothing to say. *Sorry for shoving you when I was young and crazy. I swear that's not who I am!* I still didn't know why I'd done it. I only knew that the fight didn't result in her murder since she wasn't killed until after I'd left the campus.

"Noema Titan," she said with a swirl of icy air from her ghostly breath. "I'd know you anywhere. But you're a wolf now..." She examined me, then reached out, her hand passing through my arm with the bite of frost.

Too many emotions throttled me and I didn't know what to say, so I went with a simple yet very important question. "Do you know who trapped you here?"

Sadness swam in her gaze. "No. I was so busy studying the new grimoire, I couldn't think of anything else but Lulu's legacy."

"Lulu?"

"The author of *The Book of Prophecies*."

Air was sucked from my lungs. Another truth, another piece of the puzzle. Did Lulu know my family? "Can I meet her?" It just slipped out. This didn't matter right now, but I couldn't help myself. I'd been patient through the woods, and that was enough for today.

Coach blinked and with the slight cock of her head said, "No, Dear. Lulu hasn't been heard from in many years." The swell of key lime pie in the air suddenly dropped as my disappointment replaced it. Another lead dashed.

After a hard swallow, I directed the conversation back to the important questions. "Do you know of anyone who would have wanted to kidnap you? Or kill you?"

"Kill me?"

I licked my lips and delivered the news. "Your bones were found, and the police officially determined your death a murder. We think whoever kidnapped you could be your murderer."

Coach nodded, no evidence of shock on her face. "I told my husband as much when my body was never found, and I suspected this had to be part of my remains." She glanced at the hand bones to her left. "It was the only thing that made sense, though I still don't know why anyone would have done this."

At least I knew it wasn't me... Still, did she remember me attacking her all those years ago? Unease pushed bile up my tight throat and the bitterness stained my tongue. It was fine. I was fine. *You know you're not a killer.*

Everything was not fine.

I couldn't stand it any longer. I had to know, and at least this way I got answers straight from the ghost's mouth. I forced the bile back down with a hard swallow and let the words spill out instead. "You rejected my application to Shadowvale twelve years ago on grounds of violence and then you were killed. Officer Harbour considered me a suspect until my alibi was proven. But I know I attacked you. I remember it, and I just want to say I am so, so sorry. I swear that's not me. I don't really know who I am because I turned into a werewolf and can't remember anything before. But one thing I do know is that violence is not part of who I am. Truly, I don't even squash spiders." Everything tumbled out at once in a rushed and nearly unintelligible explanation.

"Attacked..." It was all she said, her breath leaving me with chills. My chest heaved and I nearly shifted into my wolf form, ready to sprint. "Yes, I remember your application. It wasn't me who rejected it, though. Lulu did." My lips parted, but I said nothing. All the words had already come out of me, and I was left empty. "She exaggerated something about violence because that is an immediate rejection. We have enough to worry about with unstable magic and hunters who still hate supernatural beings, so any show of aggressive behavior is grounds for rejection or expulsion at Shadowvale." A funny little smile crossed her face, and I didn't know how to feel. Was it from pity? I couldn't smell a ghost.

"Exaggerated?" I repeated. I knew it. I wasn't violent then and I wasn't violent now—not even as a rowdy werewolf.

"I never knew why she did it. Lulu said she couldn't tell me, and then she turned in her resignation and I never heard from her again. If I'm recalling the details correctly, I believe that's why you pushed me. It was a very long time ago, but I remember Lulu wanted you gone. You thought I sent her away and somehow cut off communication between you two."

So many questions took my mind hostage, I couldn't settle on one to ask next. But it didn't matter because a horrible sound ripped through the air and sucked the words from my mouth.

A gunshot rang out sharp and sudden in the silent night. My ears went from perked to folded back in an instant, and a whimper escaped me. "Did you hear that?" Coach only stared at me for a moment before offering a small shake of her head. "A gun was fired. And I think the sound came from Shadowvale."

"Hunters use guns." Her face twisted. "My students...I'm not there to protect them." Sadness hung heavy in her voice.

"Actually the campus is empty. Almost." I shook my head, remembering the one person still there. The one person I'd wanted to blame this crime on from the beginning. "Madam Rowena is there. Do you think the person who did this to you is a hunter?"

Her hands shot to her mouth and her form flickered. Coach was weak, possibly due to the ghost trap. "I don't know." The erratic image of her spirit made her look as sick as a spirit could get. "Are you telling me my killer still has not been found?"

The air thickened, and a shiver shuddered down the nodes of my spine. "No."

"Then she could be in danger. She'll need help, and I am weak from this trap—"

"I can run fast."

That was all she needed to hear. Coach raised a faint, flickering hand, and the last thing I heard was her breathy request.

"Go."

CHAPTER 17
BAIT AND TWIST

COACH TOLD me to leave her behind as I bolted. I was faster on four legs, but I couldn't shift until I knew what kind of help Madam Rowena needed. If she needed me to call an ambulance, my paws wouldn't be able to fumble over a telephone well enough. And though I could manage a few words around my wolf tongue, there was no way the emergency operator would understand me over the phone.

So I pushed forward on two legs, running and running until I broke out of the other side of the forest. Fire raged in my lungs. I heaved and pushed on. The burning didn't stop when I made it to the towering double doors. The muscles in my arms protested as I dragged the heavy door open, and the hinges groaned an unwelcome greeting.

Inside, the air was icy. A shiver trickled through me, and goosebumps pricked my arms. Ghosts wailed high-pitched and desperate and painful enough that I had to fold my wolf ears back. I frowned and scanned the unrecognizable hallway.

I sucked in a breath, but the chill hurt my lungs and left my throat cold. I crept down the hallway in the general direction of the offices, hoping the shifting hallways would change and let me find them.

I'm here to help. Can't you see I'm clearly not a hunter? Absentmindedly, I wiggled my wolf ears, but the ghost's sharp cries had me quickly folding them back down against my head.

"Turn back."

I caught the jumbled words of their cries and my heart sped up. "I'm not a hunter," I said.

"Run."

"You will die."

I swallowed hard, not liking the sound of that. Were the ghosts threatening to kill me? Or were they wailing about danger from the gunshot? "Jane?" I said, voice shaking. "It's just Noema. I'm Hattie's friend, remember? I heard a gunshot and came to help. Can you tell me where Madam Rowena is?" No response. Either she wasn't nearby, or she was ignoring me. Maybe she didn't believe me. With every step, the air grew colder as ghosts huddled in around me, slowly stepping through the walls. More than a dozen ghosts surrounded me, and the temperature dropped so low, it hurt to breathe. "I swear I'm not a hunter."

The ghost in front of me opened her mouth too wide. It was a haunting sight, and the noise that came out was even worse.

I cringed, squeezing my eyes shut. "Please! Jane knows me. I was here with her friend, another ghost named Hattie June—"

The wailing stopped, Jane's grainy voice replacing it. "We are not true ghosts."

I furrowed my brow, finally perking my wolf ears. Hadn't Hattie said something similar? I'd brushed her off then. "What?"

"These are the warnings of banshees," she said.

"I don't understand." I'd never met a banshee before.

"When death is near, we step into our true form to protect Shadowvale and warn of the impending end."

My pulse thumped in my ears, heart beating faster and faster as she explained. "I heard a gunshot..." I forced words through the squeeze in my throat. "Is she—"

"Madam Rowena is dead."

Breath left my lungs. I mustered enough to squeak a single word. "Who?"

Jane's eyes dropped to the floor, and the other banshees pressed in closer. Frost ringed the wooden floorboards, and my breath came out in short, icy swirls. It was beyond cold now. If I didn't find my way out of the maze soon, I'd become a block of ice, frozen in time like the massive wolf statue in the gardens.

"Whoever is here repels us; we cannot be near them without withering. Not until they rid themselves of the repellant, and mark my words, if they ever do find themselves without repellant, we will make them suffer for what they did to Coach."

Another chill struck my spine at the venom in her voice. Jane was ready for revenge. But what repelled them? Were banshees affected by the same thing as ghosts? Silver kept ghosts away. Hattie once told me about a boost in silver jewelry sales back when supernatural creatures first came out of hiding in the 1970s. "Does silver repel banshees?" I asked. Jane nodded.

Silver. Anyone could slip on a silver ring or carry a silver spoon. But the maze spell indicated a nearby weapon, or a hunter. Did the killer wield a silver knife? No, they carried a gun. Who wanted to kill Madam Rowena, and why now? She was working on a temporary protection spell, and the protection spell's original grimoire also triggered this whole investigation. The person with the most motive to stop the spell was a hunter.

"What about her familiar? Is Mysty here?" I asked. "She can help me track the halls."

"Mysty is gone. She stopped responding to Madam Rowena. She's been trained by someone else. I only know because she left her post and abandoned her witch hours ago."

The wolf left the woman she bonded? I almost didn't believe it until...until it all made sense. There was only one other person who'd be able to make it past Mysty for access to Ted's spell. One person with a rare affinity for wild animals.

"Professor Holden," I breathed. He had the silver tooth to ward off harassment from the ghosts. But he was a teacher here; he'd been vetted and considered a safe person for Shadowvale's campus.

Or maybe he hadn't...maybe like me, he'd been rejected. Unlike my rejection, the claims of his violence might be true. Maybe I'd been right all along, Coach was killed over a rejection, it just wasn't mine. It was a crazy theory and not something I needed to spend time weaving together. I could figure out the "why" behind his cruelty later. "Can you lead me to Coach's office? I need to call the police."

"You will die."

"Run, Wolf."

The banshees shrieked their warnings again until Jane quieted them with a raised hand. "I cannot lead you there; she has warded the office against us. I can only warn you, the danger is still here. The killer is among us."

My blood ran cold. Too cold. Too slow. My heart rate dropped with the chill. I needed to get away from these banshees and call the police so they could catch the murderer before he struck again. I'd have to run and hope that the halls cooperated.

I had to get out of here and get to the police. I couldn't navigate the changing hallways, but I had to try to find an exit.

Jane seemed to understand me because she stepped aside and the other banshees followed, melting back into the walls. The chill receded, if only slightly, but it was enough for me to move my feet. They'd parted like a sea of the dead so that I could pass through.

I jogged ahead, unable to take deep breaths, unable to break into a full run. *Call the police, and get the heck out of here before Professor Holden decided to hunt me too.* My heart ached for Madam Rowena. She may have been a liar, and I'd never find out why, but she didn't deserve to be murdered in cold blood.

Sight of the faculty offices gave me a jolt of hope, and the whiff of key lime pie soothed my vibrating nerves. Spotting Coach's office with the door wide open, I picked up the pace, breaking into a run. In the doorway, my foot caught on something heavy and warm, and I slapped my hand over my mouth.

Madam Rowena lay just beyond the threshold, remnants of magic alight at her fingertips. Tendrils of her magic were slowly fading. Like embroidery threads, they were thin and wispy, with each one a different color. Blood seeped from her shoulder where she'd been shot, but she didn't smell like death. Other than the sticky smell of blood, I caught a whiff of... anger? The stinging odor of smoke didn't come from my emotions because I wasn't mad. The smell drifted up from Madam Rowena.

If she was mad, that meant she was alive.

I dropped to my knees in front of her and put my ear to her mouth. Weak breaths puffed from between her parted lips.

"Hang on, Madam Rowena," I said. "I'm going to call an ambulance."

I straightened but stopped halfway at the sound of her faint voice. "He'll kill you." I fell to her side again as she spoke. "I told Coach he was untrustworthy. All those years ago, I told her."

"Why did she hire him?" I couldn't help asking. Curiosity's peppermint aroma permeated the air.

She shook her head and winced, reaching with her good arm to put pressure on the wound with magical threads. Based on her steady breaths, her strength was slowly returning. "Because we'd never met someone with as much knowledge of magical animals and familiars. Not even witches and warlocks with familiars knew what he knew. We needed that knowledge to create stronger bonds and to protect the wild animals with magic from hunters. He proved himself a brilliant teacher, though he could never have magic of his own."

Never have magic of his own. Except for the magic he siphoned from familiars. I glanced at my hand as if the ink smudges were still there. That was why he'd drawn a spell on his hand. He was practicing with the magic he'd siphoned. That was why he killed Coach—the most powerful witch with the most powerful familiars. His role as a helpful teacher here was all a lie. His purpose. His identity even. And I knew all about confused identities. He wasn't a teacher; he was a hunter ready to use witches' own familiars against them.

Madam Rowena groaned and laid her head back again, snapping me from my thoughts. I hopped to my feet and carefully stepped over her, darting to the phone on Coach's desk. I dialed the emergency line and requested an immediate response from the paramedics with a quick warning about the banshees and, of course, the killer.

"You have to run, Noema," she said when I hung up. Her breathing was labored. "Get out of here before he figures out I'm not dead and comes back to finish the job. He knows I'm the only one with enough power to cast a temporary protection spell."

"I'm not going to leave you to die."

"Don't be stupid," she snapped.

"Too late," I said, knowing I should have listened to my gut when I'd wanted Sett to come here with me

"You idiot, he has a silver bullet." Gently, her fingers dabbed at the gunshot wound.

"Is that what he used on you?"

Apparently she still had enough energy to roll her eyes. She was basically a grown-up, more powerful version of Alicia, annoyed with my confusion. "Silver doesn't hurt witches. So no. I realized he's bypassed the weapon trigger by disguising the bullets as his teeth."

"And he only has one silver tooth." He was saving it, likely to keep the banshees at bay.

She looked at me, brows slightly raised in an expression that hinted she was impressed that I'd noticed that. She could call me stupid all she wanted, but it wasn't true.

My gaze fell to Madam Rowena again as she propped herself on her elbows, appearing better now that she had pressure, and magic, on the wound. "Since I'm already acting stupid, I have to ask, why did you lie about how I found the bones? You were basically framing me for Coach's murder."

A little scoff escaped her. "Should have known you'd hear that. Nothing is sacred around here. Not with a school full of witches and warlocks. Everyone knows everything about everyone." I stayed quiet, brows furrowed as I waited for her to explain. "Why do you think? I wanted to redirect Officer Harbour's attention from me. I fought with Coach right before she was killed. With her cold case revived, I knew he'd uncover it eventually and I'd become his number one suspect. Everyone knew I wanted her job, but I'd never hurt her. Coach knew that, but she was missing, so you'll forgive me for my temporary lapse in judgment. I panicked. I wanted to be dean so badly, and people have killed for less before. I looked beyond guilty, and since he'd already smelled your scent at the crime scene...I just went with it. It was desperate, I'll admit."

The smell of lavender confirmed the truth. It was as faint as her breaths, but she was calm, cool, and well-collected as she confessed, relieving herself of this dishonesty once and for all. I couldn't blame her for a little panic. Not with the way Officer Harbour seemed ready to pin the crime on anyone nearby. The chief of police was desperate, and Sett was right to encourage him to step off a case that made him so emotional and unstable.

"So—" She swallowed. "I'm sorry."

"It's okay, just rest until help arrives. I'll tell the banshees—"

Footsteps echoed from the hall, catching in my wolf ears and calling all of my attention. The footsteps were solid and firm and too fast to be Sett and too slow to be a paramedic coming to save us. The only other person on campus who wasn't a banshee was Professor Holden. My heart pushed up into my throat.

Did he return to be sure Madam Rowena was dead? Or did he want something else? I glanced around the room, expecting to see the grimoire or something valuable. What did the hunter want? He'd already shot the witch to stop the protection spell. The only other thing I knew about him was that he had an interest in familiars and magical animals...

"Mysty?" he called, voice even, beckoning, and followed by a quick whistle to alert the missing wolf. "Mysty, come here girl."

People kill for what they want. Madam Rowena was right about that.

The footsteps drew closer and closer, matching the beat of my pulse as Professor Holden broke into a run. My instinct was to run, but I couldn't leave Madam Rowena helpless and alone.

I needed to think of something to draw him away from her.

Would he follow me? No, Madam Rowena was powerful; he'd let me go and focus on her. I'd have to lure him away from her.

I'd have to be bait.

An idea spawned. The relief this provided gave me just enough energy to shift into my wolf form. I dropped to all fours and padded toward the door.

"Noema?" Madam Rowena said something else, but I didn't catch it as I stepped into the hallway, emerging from the office as a full blown werewolf. If he killed Coach for magical animals, maybe that desire was enough to lure him away from the head witch. At least long enough for the emergency responders to arrive.

So if an animal familiar was what Professor Holden wanted, an animal familiar was what I'd give him. I'd become the wolf he thought he'd trained.

CHAPTER 18
THE BANSHEE BRIGADE

I STEPPED out of the office as a wolf and with the chill of banshees at my back. The spirits that haunted Shadowvale's Main Hall were close, hovering, waiting, unable to enter to office thanks to Madam Rowena's wards but also unable to press in because of silver somewhere nearby. Still, their icy presence was known in the walls deep down the hallway.

At the other end of the hall, the hunter emerged, and the banshees' presence pulsed as the silver he carried pushed them back. Professor Holden held out his gun. Was it loaded with the silver bullet? He was frozen for a moment, scrutinizing me. After a second, he stretched out his free hand, keeping the barrel of the weapon trained on me. If he discharged, the bullet would embed between my eyes and into my skull.

I refused to become another pile of bones buried on Shadowvale's campus. I had to act fast—truly *act*, but I was a screenwriter, never an actress.

I drew in a breath and lowered my head. *Act like a real wolf.* I thrust out my tongue, panting. No, the hall was cold, which meant I didn't need to pant. I drew my tongue back in, my lip catching on my canines. *Really great, Noema. You probably look like a silly and confused dog.*

Maybe that was a good thing because Professor Holden snapped his fingers as if to call me to him.

I lifted my head, perking my ears and drawing my tail up to attention. Hadn't he done that to command the armadillo? Was it some sort of minor magic he'd learned to control the familiars whose magic he so desperately wanted access to? Faint but delicious smells wafted from him. Professor Holden was feeling both excited and hopeful. The scent was a sweet combination of pies, key lime and banana cream. The bait was working, which meant my acting was sufficient. Now I had to keep it up until help arrived.

He snapped his fingers again and whistled. "Here, girl."

The casting couldn't get any easier than for a werewolf to act as a wolf. Still, unease fluttered like caged bats between my ribs. I tamped down the fear teeming in my belly and stepped forward with one paw.

"That's right," he said, snapping for a third time as he slowly approached. He smiled, both of his canines missing where the regular bullet and the silver bullet were once stored. "Good wolf." I was seriously going to puke all over this guy if he came any closer. *You can do this. There's no stage, no camera. Just be a real wolf for a few minutes.* Swallowing the bile on my tongue, I forced my tail into a slight wag as if I liked how he was talking to me. "Where's the spirit of your bonded witch, hmm?"

A magical animal would understand his words, so I let out a whine and threw my head to the side, indicating that Madam Rowena was behind me inside Coach's office. He needed to believe she was lying there dead, and that her spirit was hovering nearby. Maybe if he thought she was already a dangerous ghost, he'd leave. But that was wishful thinking, considering he inched closer and the invisible silver barrier pressed the banshees back two paces. He was trying to gain my trust so he could use a bit of my magic.

Unfortunately for him, I didn't have magic. Though I may have once been a witch, the only power I'd ever claimed came from smelling emotions. Unless he wanted to know that jealousy reeked of body odor, he was in for a whole lot of disappointment. Of course, I'd never trust him anyway, and I wasn't a familiar.

I inched forward, willing my paws to move toward the awful man despite the threat of the cold hard steel in his hands and the deadly silver within. He had to believe I was a wolf, not a werewolf.

Keep your ears perked.

Walk normally.

Would a wolf growl at a weapon?

We each took careful steps as if every move might set off a bomb. I paused where the hall branched off into shorter sections by the faculty offices. Slowly, we'd closed the distance between one another, and traces of his ammonia-soaked fear of me, or possibly his fear of wherever he believed Madam Rowena's spirit was, faded. Replacing the stench was the smell of fruit-flavored pies and a whiff of sandalwood from confidence. Okay, I could keep this up until I heard sirens.

Where the heck were the police and the ambulance anyway?

They were likely just minutes away. Maybe. Hopefully. I padded another few steps toward Professor Holden. The ruse was working. He turned his free hand over and held it out for me to sniff. But the weapon never moved. He gripped it, carefully angling it at me even when I inched forward to sniff his hand the way a wolf might under his minor magic.

Gross. His fingers stunk like he hadn't washed them. The bite of metal and sweat and a whole host of other odors came from his hand. I tried not to bare my teeth in disgust, and when I succeeded at keeping my snout shut, pride swelled within my chest between the buzz of nerves. Finally, he lowered his arm, letting the weapon point at the ground where it could do nothing more than damage the floorboards if fired. Relief washed through me. The banshees were far enough away that I could breathe without the pain of ice in my lungs, and the hunter's gun was no longer aimed between my eyes.

Hattie would be fiercely proud of my acting. I even wagged my tail when Professor Holden gingerly petted the top of my head in a weak effort to gain my trust.

A chill descended upon the side hall as the banshees moved through the walls and rooms, coming as close to the silver's barrier as possible. I caught a glimpse of their flurried limbs phasing through the wallpaper at the far end of the faculty offices.

A sharp gasp came from the office where Madam Rowena lay. Professor Holden jumped, throwing his weapon back out with both hands and gripping it until his knuckles went white. His finger paused over the trigger. Pee-soaked odors of fear rippled from him until smoky anger replaced it. He narrowed his eyes and glanced between me and the hallway.

Either Madam Rowena was struggling to breathe or the pain was getting worse. Whatever triggered the sound, it revealed she wasn't dead. A spirit didn't need to breathe, and though the sharp sound of sudden breath could be mimicked by a ghost's shock, it never sounded quite the same.

Professor Holden's gaze shifted back to me. He knew the target was still alive. That much was evident as he lost interest in me and marched forward. Without thinking, I jumped in front of him and a growl escaped me, my wolf tongue forming around the word "Stop."

"What the hell?" he said, eyes raking over me.

Curses. Real wolves don't talk.

When Professor Holden aimed the gun at me again, my heart fell to the pit of my stomach. He kept it up, trained on me as he slowly walked toward Coach's office. If he shot Madam Rowena again, she wouldn't survive. But what could I do to stop him when the weapon was loaded with a silver bullet?

Of course, he only had one. And if he discharged the silver, the banshees could have their revenge on the man who killed their beloved Coach. They could freeze him where he stood, or shock him long enough to get me and Madam Rowena out or for the paramedics to arrive.

As if this was a stage and my thoughts were the cue, a distant siren pricked my ears. They were almost here. Almost, but not close enough to stop the man marching toward his victim.

I glanced down the side hall, glimpsing the banshees within the paintings. They were hovering as close as possible, and their nervous, excited, angry energy ramped my heart rate. Before fear strangled the idea, I decided I had to take this lure to the next level. I had to get that silver away from him.

Professor Holden was almost to the door at Coach's office when I barked and bared my fangs. He pointed the gun at me and told me to shut up. "Stupid wolf."

That was my clue—my cue. He didn't recognize my attempt at speaking, which meant he still thought I was a familiar, a wolf, nothing more...powerful.

I licked my snout, readying to form my tongue around words as well as I possibly could. "I'm a werewolf." And I wouldn't dare let anyone get away with calling me stupid for the second time today.

His fear spiked and permeated the hallway with a horrible odor. Sure he had a silver bullet, but for a man who worked at Shadowvale, I had no doubt he knew that a single bullet probably wouldn't stop me from mauling him to death before the bullet killed me. Silver was a slow poison, and one bullet had to be perfectly aimed for the immediate take down of a werewolf as big as me.

I had to trigger him to shoot. It was now or never.

I threw my head back and howled, sending his fear over the edge and just enough to push him to pull the trigger. I lunged into the side hall at the sound of the gun cracking. The exploding weapon was like a bite to my wolf ears—too loud, painful. Everything was deafened and distant, like I was hearing the screaming, piercing wail of the banshees from miles away. In the seconds that followed, I collapsed in the side hall, my own fear buckling my knees while a dozen shrieking banshees phased through the rooms and walls as they descended upon Professor Holden.

Jane and the others swept past me, giving me a wide enough berth that the chill only left me with a few shivers. Our eyes connected for half a second. I tried to bob my head in a faint sign of gratitude. With a blink, she focused her attention on the killer. She surged forward, screeching at him with a warning that could make ears bleed. I slumped against the wall, desperate to catch my breath and slap my hands over my ears.

Sirens drew closer, splitting through the wailing. Wailing that warned of death to come—possibly Professor Holden's death.

Despite the chaos, my mind quieted. Safe and alone in the hallway where I'd first met Coach, an idea struck me. What if a ghost overcame the odds of death's amnesia and solved her own murder?

Finally, and at the strangest time, I had an idea for my screenplay.

CHAPTER 19
A+ ARREST

SHADOWVALE WAS TEEMING with police officers again. Once Sett arrived, Holden was promptly arrested and thrown into the back of a squad car, where he shouted and spat from behind the barred windows.

"She lies!" Holden's face bloomed beet red. The closed door muffled his screams. "Coach is a liar!"

"Hey." Sett gently knocked on the window. "Give it a rest. We matched your handwriting to the inscription on her bones, buddy. It's over."

It was over. I wanted to howl a thank you to the heavens.

I sat beside one of the tall columns that flanked the front steps, waiting for Sett as he spoke with Officer Harbour. It felt good to catch my breath after pulling a true all-nighter. I pulled Sett's massive coat tighter around me as the night's frigid air lingered into the morning.

After retrieving my clothes and gathering enough energy to shift into my human form and get dressed, I was still chilly, so Sett had offered his navy jacket. It dwarfed me, but at least it kept me warm after the icy effect of the banshees.

Sett sat down beside me, his arm bumping into mine. I

found myself leaning into him as he explained what he uncovered when he went to clear up the faulty arrest on Doctor Leek. It'd all happened so fast. When they released Doctor Leek and escorted her through the station, she saw the forensic specialist dusting Coach's bones. "Her understanding of summoning clued her in on the odd markings. That was when Carissa Harbour's spirit arrived at the station to get help after hearing a gun fire on campus. She'd confirmed what Doctor Leek found."

After Coach regained her strength, she went straight to the police station, where she was able to identify Holden's handwriting on her own bones. The inscription was so small and so faint, it'd taken days of carefully brushing off dirt and dust to uncover it without marring the bones. They finally had solid proof of Holden's attempt to summon her spirit the lazy way. And when it didn't work on the spirit of the most powerful witch to have lived, he used the student's new summoning theories.

Having the whole story felt good. Well, almost the whole story.

I craned my neck, eyeing Holden through the squad car's rear window, then turned to Sett. "Why did Holden hang around for so long when he'd failed to get rid of Coach? Why not try to get magic in some easier way?" Twenty years was a long time to wait. As much work as I put into learning patience, I'd *never* be that patient.

Sett's forced breath swirled in a white puff in front of him. "He was in a hunter's clan—a whole illegal organization of supernatural killers." A chill settled over the back of my neck. I ducked lower in the safety of Sett's coat so Holden couldn't see me. "Coach told us that her mentor, another very powerful witch, had humiliated this hunter's clan. We suspect Holden was a hunter who tried to kill Coach's mentor. But he was young and brand new to the hunter's clan back then. When he failed to kill her, he got kicked out of the organization. This murder came from his misplaced vengeance after he couldn't find Coach's mentor. Holden's defeat revealed his weakness as a hunter in front of his clan, so he wanted revenge. He wanted to use a witch's own magic against her. It seems that along the way, he became obsessed with the magic itself."

I shook my head. "I doubt it was an addiction to magic. More likely the power he felt *from* the magic. Senna said they have a whole course on not becoming power-hungry once their abilities become more potent."

He hummed his agreement as my attention slid to another very powerful witch.

On the opposite side of the gravel driveway sat Madam Rowena. She perched at the back of an ambulance, her legs dangling over the edge with Mysty at her feet. Her beloved familiar had been smart enough to run from Professor Holden's influence. Half-bonded to him, she must have been at war with herself, wanting to protect Madam Rowena but feeling the need to obey Professor Holden.

Apparently, the wolf was halfway to the police station when Sett and Officer Harbour spotted her along the highway and brought her back here. Mysty growled at the poor paramedic attempting to help Madam Rowena. When the paramedic took white gauze out of a plastic package, Madam Rowena tore it from her hands and insisted on finishing the bandages herself. She was truly a force, having removed the bullet herself, and tied a makeshift tourniquet made out of the shredded pieces of my Shadowvale T-shirt around her shoulder. I couldn't imagine the pain she was in from the gunshot, but it might have been better if she'd waited until after I'd lured the killer away from her to remove it.

Now that the paramedics had properly cleaned the wound, Madam Rowena shooed them away. Clearly the head witch was also the most stubborn witch, which was a good thing, considering she was stubborn enough to refuse to succumb to the wound.

Madam Rowena must have felt my gaze because she looked up from the bandages and met my eyes. She lifted her chin in acknowledgment, and I returned the gesture with a small smile. I wanted nothing more than to run over to her and beg for her to interpret the spells and prophecies in *The Book of Prophecies* for me. But now wasn't the time, and Coach was the witch in charge of the grimoire's study, not Madam Rowena.

I could only hope they'd resume studying it, and that I'd learn more about Lulu and the family who wrote it. Maybe if Coach didn't agree to study the magic, she'd help me track down the author and the others mentioned in the prophecies. Coach and Madam Rowena would help a former Shadowvale hopeful, right? It was selfish to think so, but I couldn't help wanting more answers. The more I'd learned about my past and my identity, the less it seemed I understood.

Holding a smile, I nodded at Madam Rowena to suggest I'd forgiven her for trying to pawn the crime off on me. Desperate times, after all. I didn't blame her.

The crisp air smelled of autumn despite the fact that spring semester was in full swing and February was just around the corner. Shadowvale was in an eternal fall, surrounded by the forest's shadows and permeated with witches' magic. I soaked in the faint aroma of apples and the hint of Sett's signature sourdough smell.

"I'm ready to get on the road whenever you are. I know you're missing the kids."

My heart squeezed. It felt like months since I'd hugged Stevie or listened to Jovi relay facts he learned from a book. I couldn't wait to kick a soccer ball around with Dio and Halen and bask in Mockbuster's signature smell: chocolate and popcorn.

"What about your offer to help Caldale police department?" I twisted and looked up at him. I knew investigations didn't end as soon as the criminal was in handcuffs. Paperwork and processing were the tedious sides that I believed Sett secretly loved. He could take his sweet time with every form.

"With Holden in custody, I've told Officer Harbour I'm stepping down from the help I've offered. He wants to take the lead again. Now that his wife's spirit is safely at home, she's decided to retire from Shadowvale."

My mouth fell open. Coach was retiring? I snuck a glance across the gravel at Madam Rowena. Would she become the next dean? Maybe now I only had to convince one person to resume studying the grimoire.

Sett descended the steps and I stood, wiping the dust off my pants. We'd nearly reached Sett's car when another vehicle sped through the iron gate and rolled to a stop in a puff of dust. From the driver's seat, Ted pointed at us, his other hand still on the steering wheel. Senna hopped out of the passenger side and ran around the car before throwing her arms around my neck.

"Noema!" she shouted. I maneuvered from under her hug so that I could position myself to return the embrace. "It feels so good to know it'll be safe around here again."

Both happiness's and love's delightful scents emanated from her, mixing with the fresh smell of her body lotion. When we pulled apart, the beaming smile on her face matched the smells of giddiness.

"How did you already hear it was safe to return?" I asked.

"The banshees stopped wailing," she said. "We could hear them from our hotel when we were trying to sleep. Not that Ted and I slept a lot." The scent of love wafted from her.

I glanced between them as he emerged from the car. "Are you and Ted an item again?"

Senna drew in a long breath and fingered the bead at the bottom of one of her many braids. Finally, she released the breath before flashing him a dazzling smile. "Yeah, yeah I think we are."

Sett knocked his knuckles against the top of the car, drawing my attention from my friend. His slate eyes shifted between us, and then he mustered an apologetic smile. "Noema, we've got to get on the road before I'm too tired to drive."

I nodded. "We'll hurry." To my rescue, Madam Rowena strode up to Sett and thrust out her hand. She thanked him for explaining her innocence to the Caldale police. With him distracted, I turned back to Senna. "Are you going to be okay after all this?"

She nodded. "I'm definitely freaked about Professor Holden. I mean, we all trusted him. It's freaking wild that he was a hunter. But I just want life to get back to normal now so that I can be done with my senior spell. Once presentation day is over and I'm three shots of vodka deep, then I'll be okay."

I laughed. "Good. And Professor Holden is in custody now." I pointed at the squad car where Professor Holden slumped in the back seat. "He was so desperate for magic, he tried siphoning it from the familiars."

"This is seriously wild, but it totally makes sense that he'd want Coach's familiars since they're, like, insanely powerful. Like who wouldn't want a spider that's a straight gateway to ancient magic?" She mimicked the act of an explosion coming out of her head. Once Ted joined her, they said something I couldn't hear, both of them huddled together and gaping at the professor who'd killed their dean and tried to kill the head witch. After a moment, she spun around with a frown twisting her mouth again. "So what did he want with *The Book of Prophecies*? It doesn't include much about familiars that I've heard."

"Other than summoning? My guess is it was to stop the recreation of the protection spell. He killed in an attempt to take a witch's familiars before, which means he might try it again. But if Madam Rowena cast the protection spell on Shadowvale, he wouldn't have the chance."

"But the spell isn't even in the book anymore."

"No, but the clues are. At least that's what Madam Rowena once told me. There might be enough for them to put it together again. Even if it is ruined."

I'd come here on the field trip hoping for more understanding of the grimoire, or the people mentioned in it, but I was leaving with more questions. At least I knew one thing: my last name, though knowing it didn't change me. Knowing past versions of me didn't change who I was now. I was still Noema —whether it was Noema Titan or Noema Wolf didn't truly matter. My smoky frustration gave way to a peaceful lemon scent.

"I'm sorry we didn't find any information on your mark or your family," she said, understanding my expression. I probably looked lost, defeated, or maybe just overtired and a little hungry. That pizza was too many hours ago. Maybe Sett would agree to stop for pancakes at a diner along the highway. The thought of syrup and sausage boosted my spirit.

"It's okay. But I wouldn't hate it if you dropped a few hints about it to Madam Rowena—after your senior spells, of course."

She grinned. "Definitely."

For once the impatient one, Sett prodded me. "Noema."

I turned and nodded before giving Senna another quick hug. Once I wished her luck on her senior spell, I climbed into the passenger seat and sank into the cushion, finally allowing myself to rest.

WHEN I DOZED, Sett turned down the radio and let me drift into a full nap. We stopped at a Denny's diner and wolfed down two plates of a sunrise breakfast order. He explained the evidence he'd found in the case paperwork. Information about Professor Holden's first arrest that led Sett to track him to a group of illegal hunters.

I nodded along, swallowing a gulp of orange juice. "The banshees mentioned that both he and Madam Rowena had trouble with the law before."

Sett stared at the ice melting in his glass, a thoughtful crease between his brow. "That's what I was telling you about back at Shadowvale. Madam Rowena's arrest had to do with a peaceful protest that exploded with unstable magic." He explained Professor Holden's motive again now that I was awake and able to process the details. "He confessed that a witch once showed him up in front of his group of hunters. Essentially, they embarrassed him, and he wanted to get his revenge by stealing their magic."

I ate and listened and ate some more while he talked. Shock had me responding like Senna. "Freaking wild. I'm speechless that a hunter would go through all that just to get a little magic."

He laughed. "You can't be speechless and talk at the same time."

I smirked and responded by tapping my finger to my lips. The joy quickly deflated when another question popped in my mind. "What about my fur at the crime scene? Officer Harbour said it was from my summer coat, but I was never here over the summer. Someone had to have taken my fur and staged it inside that trunk."

Sett swallowed a bite of his breakfast burrito and put it back on his plate. "It is as I suspected. You were framed, just not by Professor Holden."

"That doesn't make any sense."

He shook his head, eyes dropped to his plate as he stared thoughtfully. "No, it doesn't." He lifted his gaze and held mine. The understanding between us was steady, comfortable. Though we were still miles from home, it felt like I was already there. "We'll find out the truth."

Hope and sadness and love burned behind my eyes. I forced myself to look away before he caught sight of my tears and worried.

We'll *find out the truth.* Together.

CHAPTER 20
PROPHETIC PROPOSAL

AT HOME, I gathered all four kids into a hug before we collapsed on the couch. We watched hours of Disney movies until Squeaks drifted off to sleep and we all followed him to dreamland one-by-one, snoring into the night. I woke to a distant ring that caught in my wolf ears.

Downstairs, Mockbuster's phone rang and rang and rang. I untangled myself from blankets, stuffed animals, and pillows, tiptoeing through the maze of passed-out pups. The ringing blared louder with every step I descended into the shop. Dawn light streamed in through the glass walls at the front of Mockbuster.

I plucked the phone from the receiver on the wall and said hello.

"Noema?" a woman's voice said. "It's Madam Rowena."

"Is everything okay?"

"I've been going through what I can salvage from the grimoire and studying the pieces all night. I can tell you something that might be of interest to you."

My wolf ears perked and my pulse sped. What had they discovered? A million thoughts surfaced at once, tangling with one another. Did it somehow reveal who'd framed me all those years ago? No, the killer was caught. My fur found on an old trunk was of no interest to anyone but me. "Go on."

"There is a prophecy that I've been able to connect with the Titan family. Not the same prophecy that mentions you—another one. It is called the Guide's Wives, and it's about reapers." The tornado of thoughts came to a sudden halt, but the quiet wasn't calming. In my mind's eye, I saw Crow's face, his messy overgrown hair, his smirk and hooked scar. He was the reaper I knew best, so of course he popped into my mind. But why did my heart skip at the thought of him? "The prophecy says that every witch in the Titan family is fated to marry a reaper. Together they're stronger and can lead spirits with unfinished business to rest. So I don't know what that all means for you, but Senna told me you were desperate for breadcrumbs."

Breadcrumbs. I *was* hungry when I'd ask her to drop hints. "Oh." It was all I could say.

"I'll let you know more about your witch ancestry when I dig deeper into the grimoire. For now, we'll be spending most of our focus to figure out how these spells led to the creation of the protection spell. It could be months before you hear from me again, though, so don't get your hopes up."

I cleared my throat and managed a creaky "thank you" before she hung up. In a daze, I hooked the phone back on the receiver and sank into the seat behind the shop's register. I perched at the edge of the stool and stared at the floor, a mess of questions and strange emotions. The Guide's Wives prophecy was the last thing I expected to hear about. I never gave it much attention when I'd had the grimoire in my care. It didn't seem to relate to me the way the other prophecies had. But I was a witch and I was a Titan, so I was also fated to marry a reaper.

Crow would be returning soon. He'd left me a message on

my answering machine that he'd be back today, but I didn't know if I could bear to see him. Though he wouldn't know about the prophecy—about my fate—I'd still feel awkward. I'd probably trip over my own two feet in front of him or accidentally spill my Diet Pepsi all over his black clothes.

"Fated to marry a reaper," I whispered aloud. Crow was fun, adventurous, even a little dangerous the way he encouraged me to do whatever I wanted—and as an impulsive, impatient werewolf, doing whatever I wanted was inherently dangerous. But could I spend my life with him? Would he be a father to my kids? I couldn't picture it because he wasn't exactly the fatherly type. He was too carefree and spontaneous for school schedules and soccer practices.

Movement outside caught the corner of my eye, and my head snapped up. It wasn't a Mockbuster customer or my ghost best friend from next door. Sett's large frame filled the other side of the glass doorway, likely headed to the police station across town. He wore the coat I'd borrowed. The one that nearly swallowed me like an oversized blanket. Through the glass door, he met my gaze and offered a little wave. I lifted my hand and returned the greeting, my lips curling into a small smile. He tapped his fingers to his lips. When I copied the little gesture that'd become a silent understanding between us, he cracked a knowing smile, one shared just between us. I was never quiet, and apparently, he liked that.

Heat flared in the curve of my cheeks, and I covered my blush with my palms. Sett didn't need to see how he affected me—how he shouldn't be affecting me when I hadn't talked to Crow in days. I glanced at the ticking watch at my wrist. Crow had given it to me so I could keep track of the time between when we'd see each other again. Maybe he hoped I wouldn't forget him while he was out reaping lost spirits.

Confusion swirled in the air around me, spicy and sweet

like a pineapple pizza, as I watched Sett disappear down the sidewalk. I sucked in a sharp breath that sliced through my lungs with a jolt of pain.

I wouldn't hear from Madam Rowena for months. Answers were finally on the horizon, but the horizon was about a million miles away. Patience was my least favorite virtue and one that often slipped from my grasp. I stood and wandered the aisles of movies, considering what all my favorite heroines might do in this situation..

Finally, I landed on an idea. I'd throw myself into a project as a distraction. As Hattie worked on securing funding for Everland Theater's transformation, I resolved to have a screen-play ready before then to play on the big screen. Even if the presentation of it would only be a home video recorded on Halen's camcorder, it was a start. And like the study of *The Book of Prophecies*, I had to start small.

Maybe, now that I knew I was a witch, I could learn a little magic that'd bring the screenplay to life. My ears folded back.

I'm a witch. A witch fated to marry a reaper.

I'd been so obsessed with my past, I never thought the grimoire—even if it was full of prophecies—would reveal my future.

JOIN NOEMA FOR ANOTHER ENCHANTING MYSTERY IN *VAMPIRES, VCRS, AND VIOLENCE: BOOK 5 OF THE BEWITCHER'S BEACH PARANORMAL COZY MYSTERIES!*

Please consider leaving a review at your favorite place to purchase books! Also, a share with your friends who love to laugh and solve mysteries would be greatly appreciated. My quest as an author is to make others feel seen through the adventure of fiction. Please reach out to me and let me know if my stories have touched you. You, dear reader, are who this book was written for.

BEWITCHER'S BEACH RECIPES

COLLEGE DORM EDITION

(Everything is easy enough to cook in a college dorm room!)

JOVI'S ENGLISH MUFFIN PIZZA

When to eat: whenever you're craving a slice, but don't have the extra cash to get delivery. Plus, it's better than frozen pizza—though Noema still prefers the ease of frozen foods. Maybe someday Sett will convince her otherwise. It's little Jovi who wants to learn to cook from Sett, and this recipe is what he'll try first.

Ingredients:

- 1 jar of pizza sauce
- A package of fresh English muffins
- Mozzarella cheese
- (Optional) toppings: pepperoni, olives, spinach, mushrooms, etc.

Instructions:

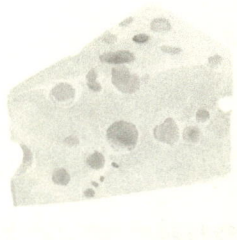

- Preheat the toaster oven to 350 degrees.
- Spread pizza sauce on the insides of the English muffin like butter. Keep it light to avoid a soggy crust.
- Shred Mozzarella cheese and top the English muffin generously.
- Add toppings.
- Bake for about 10 minutes.
- Devour—and get rid of that hangover!

SENNA'S BROWNIE IN A MUG

When to eat: after you've enjoyed some nutritious food and need a sweet treat! Or whenever you're craving it...maybe 1:00 am? If you're up that late, be sure to tell Noema if you see anything suspicious. And don't let the banshees bother you.

Ingredients:

- 2 Tbsp. butter
- 2 Tbsp. plus 1 tsp. granulated sugar
- 3 Tbsp. cocoa powder
- 1/4 tsp. instant espresso powder
- Pinch of salt
- 2 1/2 Tbsp. whole milk or water
- 2 Tbsp. all-purpose flour
- 1 Tbsp. mini chocolate chips, plus more for topping

- 1/2 tsp. peanut butter, or other nut butter (optional)

Instructions:

- Heat butter in a microwave-safe mug until melted.
- With a fork, mix in sugar, cocoa powder, espresso powder, and salt.
- Whisk in milk and mini chocolate chips.
- Add peanut butter on the top (optional).
- Add more mini chocolate chips on the top.
- Microwave for 1 minute.
- Let cool, AND DO NOT FEED TO WEREWOLVES! All others, enjoy.

LULU'S LOADED SWEET POTATO

When to eat: before a party! Load up on something substantial before you'll be out all night. Of course, this hearty little meal is good at any time.

Created by Lulu for her daughters.

Ingredients:

- 1 sweet potato
- Desired toppings (pick and choose): 1 can black beans, shredded cheese, sour cream, avocado, salsa, tomato, green onions, etc.
- Spices (optional): chili powder, ground cumin.

Instructions:

- Wash and pierce sweet potato with a fork.
- Microwave sweet potato for 3 minutes, then turn to the other side and microwave for another 2 minutes until tender. Pierce with a fork to determine tenderness. Cook time may depend on the size of the potato as well as the microwave power. Let the potato take a nap (I mean, rest for 2 minutes so it isn't piping hot!)
- While waiting, rinse black beans and cook in the microwave for 30 seconds - 1 minute, until heated.
- Shred cheese/chop onions/dice tomatoes/cut avocados.
- Slice the potato open and pinch spices.
- Add desired toppings.
- Eat immediately for a warm and cozy meal!

ABOUT THE AUTHOR

Congenital Heart Defect survivor, Emily Fluke, finds joy and peace through the expression of writing. She is a firm believer that all stories need a little magic and a lot of excitement. Emily and her husband spend their free time wrangling two children and playing video games in their busy California lifestyle. Otherwise, you'll find Emily solving an escape room, running, or writing Magic the Gathering-based poetry.

To stay up to date on new releases and connect with me, visit my website at Emilyfluke.com or follow me on social media under Author Emily Fluke, or @emilyflukefairytales.